CRUSHED

By

ANDREA SMITH

Copyright © 2016

Http://www.andreasmithauthor.com/

Beth -
Give this
one a try!

1

INTRODUCTION

I have fallen in love with YA/NA Romance and Suspense. I got the idea for "Crushed" from something that happened many years ago, to someone I knew very well. I hope you enjoy the story.

This is Book 1 in the "Evermore Series." It is a serial meaning that each novella needs to be read in order for the complete story.

1) Crushed   July2016

2) Claimed   August 2016

3) Paparazzi   September 2016

4) Star F*cking   October 2016

TABLE OF CONTENTS

Crushed

by Andrea Smith

Meatball Taster Publishing, LLC.

ACKNOWLEDGMENTS

Edited by: Ashley Blaschak Stout

Formatted by: Erik Gevers

Cover Design: Frina Art

PROLOGUE

I awoke instantly as soon as I heard the sound of shattering glass from the kitchen. I glanced over at the clock on my nightstand. It was only six in the morning. My alarm wouldn't go off for another hour.

I knew what the noise was; no cause for alarm. Mama was still up. She'd been on a three-day bender, during which time anything could happen.

I pulled the covers back, and tiptoed across the bare wooden floor to the door of my bedroom. It was right off the kitchen. Actually, I think its intended use had been a large pantry. Our apartment was one of two on the lower floor of an old Victorian house that had been chopped up to make apartments in the older side of town.

I opened my bedroom door, and there was Mama. Staggering around, looking for a broom to sweep up the shattered amber-colored glass that was strewn all over the worn linoleum floor. She saw me, and immediately flailed her arms my way.

"Go on back to bed, Neely," she said, her words slurred. "You don't need to be coming out here in your bare feet, stepping all over this mess and getting cut now, hear?"

"What happened?" I asked, my eyes squinting trying to adjust to the glare of the overhead lighting.

"Well, what do you think happened, girl? That damn liquor store filled this bottle with bourbon, not scotch like it was supposed to be. As if I can't tell the difference 'tween the two. I'll take care of Mr. McGreedy first thing when he opens his store today, I'll tell you that! Now go on, I got this covered. Go on back to bed."

There was no use arguing with Mama when she got this way. To do so would most likely end up with me having a split lip or bruised cheek. Mama was a soft and gentle person, except when she was hitting the bottle.

It wasn't always this way.

I climbed back into my bed, and pulled the covers up to my chin. I could hear her clanging around in the kitchen, muttering profanities that I'd never dare use in front of her and then, eventually, the sobs of her desperation floated into my room.

Her binges were getting longer and occurring more often. I knew the pressure of everything was taking a toll on her.

I wasn't sure how much longer things could go on like this. She'd just lost her fourth job in as many months for attendance.

We barely survived on the child support my father was sending monthly. My grandparents had bailed us out at first, but that only lasted about six months before they'd had it and told Mama to clean up her act. And to find her own damn place.

So we'd become estranged. Well, at least Mama had, but as she said, "We're a package deal, Neely. If they've shut me out, than they've shut us both out, as far as I'm concerned."

We'd moved to a small town about twenty miles from the small town where my grandparents lived because Mama said she wasn't about to live her life in a fish bowl and feel their judgment from around the corner.

And now one of them was gone.

I laid in the dark, chewing on my bottom lip. Sleep wouldn't be returning anytime soon. My tiredness would evaporate soon enough, only to be replaced by concern and worry.

At seventeen, I was already learning a valuable lesson, mostly about pride. They say it 'goeth before the fall,' and that I truly believed.

My mother hadn't hit rock bottom just yet.

But she was so damn close, I knew there'd be no turning back now. It was up to me to do what she couldn't bring herself to do for her own good.

But I wasn't sure whether I had the guts to do it.

CHAPTER 1

Four Years Prior
August 5, 1992
Malibu, CA

"Toss it over here, Neely," Seth yelled, holding his arms up waiting for me to throw the Nerf football to him on the other end of the pool. "Bet you can't lob it that far," he challenged, treading water in the deep end.

"Oh yeah?" I challenged. "I can throw better than you can, Seth Drake," I hollered back, raising my right arm and hurling it over his head. It bounced off of the diving board, and landed in the grass behind the pool.

"The thing is," Seth yelled, "precision requires more skill than velocity."

He always said things like that when I outdid him on something. Seth was just that way.

"Neilah Grace Evans," my mother yelled from the patio door, "time for you to get on outta there and get ready for dinner. Your daddy's taking us out tonight for dinner at the Pier."

"Okay, Mama," I hollered back, swimming over towards the ladder.

"*Okay Mama*," Seth mimicked. "When you gonna lose that hillbilly accent, *Neilah Grace*?" he asked, trying to talk Southern. He failed miserably.

"Never, ever," I said, grabbing a towel from the chair. "My roots can show every bit as much as those bleached blondes on television. At least I'm for real."

He chuckled, displaying a dimple. Seth was fourteen, a year older than me, but we'd been hanging out together ever since my family had moved here from Nashville. My father had taken a job with a new law firm, switching from the music industry to the television industry.

It had been exciting at first. Like a new adventure in a new land. But after two years, Southern California still didn't feel like home to me. I missed Nashville. My friends and my grandparents. But mostly, I missed the friendliness of the South.

Seth was practically my only friend. We lived in close proximity, went to the same school, rode the bus together, and hung out a lot. His mother was an actress on a daytime soap, and his father did something technical at the studios. Nearly everyone in Malibu had some connection to the entertainment industry but, to be honest, I wasn't all that impressed.

Sure, it was obvious there was a lot of wealth and fame in these parts, but I wasn't sure that we were as happy as we'd been in Tennessee.

At least that's how it seemed for Mama and me.

"See you tomorrow?" Seth asked, quirking a brow. "Wanna go to the beach or something?"

"Sure," I said, stepping into my flip-flops. "Just come by when you're ready."

I watched as Seth loped off toward the beach, where he would walk a fifty or sixty yard stretch before taking the path up to his house. It was huge and sprawling, larger than ours, but then he had two younger sisters at home. His family had a full-time housekeeper, too. My mother handled everything around our place except for the yard and pool. We had a guy that came weekly to handle that stuff.

"Make sure you're dried off before you come inside," I heard her call out from the dining room. "I swear, you're brown as a bean from the sun. Are you using that sunscreen I bought you?"

"Yes, Mama," I replied, rubbing my legs and feet dry. I stepped through the sliding screen door into the house. "Is this a dressed-up thing for dinner?" I asked, hoping that it wasn't. Everything in Malibu was always so overdone, so glam and glitzy.

"Just put on one of those pretty sundresses I bought you and your new sandals, sugar. But get in the shower and wash all that chlorine off your hair before it turns green again."

I was blonde, and what with the sun and swimming nearly every day, my hair had taken on a greenish hue much to Mama's dismay. She'd bought some special clarifying shampoo for me and was forever harping on me to use it after every swim.

"I swear," she continued, watering a couple of the houseplants she had located around the dining room, "that boy is sweet on you, Neely. He keeps his distance from you now, doesn't he?"

That was Mama's way of asking if he'd gotten fresh with me yet.

"He's a friend, Mama," I said, rolling my eyes. "We just hang out together, that's all. He's the only person near my age around here. You do want me to have friends, don't you?"

"Well, of course I do, but I also know at fourteen boys start getting, you know, ideas in their heads."

I felt a blush spread across my face. "Seth doesn't think of me like that, Mama. I'm going to get my shower," I finished, exiting the dining room to head towards my bathroom. It made me uncomfortable when my mother said things like that. At thirteen, I had no interest in boys…at least in *that* way.

The thing was, my junior high female classmates seemed as if they'd known each other all their lives. After two years, I still felt like the new kid. I had a feeling that I always would. Seth had been the first one to open up to me shortly after we had arrived in sun-drenched Southern California.

He'd seen me on the beach right before school was due to start and struck up a conversation. It was mostly questions on his part.

"You the new kid that moved in up there?" he asked, nodding upwards to where our house was located.

"Yep," I replied, still drawing a landscape in the wet sand with a stick I'd found.

"What's your name?"

"Neely Evans."

"How old are you?"

"Eleven."

"Got any brothers or sisters?"

"Nope."

"Any dogs or cats?"

"Nope."

"What do you do for fun then?"

That had seemed like a strange question to me. It was like I couldn't possibly have fun unless I had siblings or pets.

"Lots of things."

"Like what?"

"Like drawing and painting. I'm gonna be an artist."

Seth had laughed. *"An artist? My dad says most of them starve to death!"*

"Do not!" I snapped, clearly agitated with this strange boy who asked too many questions.

"Well I'm going to be a movie star. My mother says I'm a natural."

"A natural what?" I asked, glancing up at him from where I was crouched down trying to finish my sand art.

"A natural-born actor," he said as if I should've known that without asking. *"She's an actress. Makes lots of money, too."*

"Sounds like you're a braggart," I had replied, turning back to my masterpiece. *"Mama says it's rude to brag."*

He'd given me a frown. *"No brag, just fact,"* he replied with a shrug. *"You talk funny. Where're you from?"*

I bristled at his last comment. People out here were forever commenting that I talked funny. *"Maybe you just listen funny,"* I replied. *"And to answer your question, I'm from Earth, same as you."*

"Hardy-har-har," he replied. *"Answer my question, Neely Evans."*

I stood up, brushing the sand off of my knees. "You're awfully nosy," I commented. "What's your name?"

"Seth Drake. I live at the next house down the beach."

"Well, Seth Drake. I've answered all the questions I'm going to for now. I'm going swimming in my own pool. So I reckon you'll just have to figure the rest of it out for yourself."

I'd turned and skipped down the beach to where the wooden steps led up to our property. Just as I reached the top, I heard him yell up to me.

"I'm betting Tennessee! I'm really good at guessing accents! See you later, Tennessee!"

And that had been the start of my first real friendship in Southern California. One that would turn out to be precious, but not withstanding the distance when our lives in Malibu came to a crashing halt a few years later.

CHAPTER 2

Present Day

September 1996

My alarm went off, and just as I had anticipated, I'd not fallen back to sleep. I'd simply reflected back on our life before my mother had started her decline into misery and depression.

How was I supposed to fix her?

She'd alienated herself from everyone who'd ever loved her except for me.

She was only thirty-seven, but ever since my father and her had split nearly three years ago, things had slowly started down the path of destruction for her.

My father, an entertainment lawyer in Los
Angeles, had fallen in love with one of his clients.
One of his very rich, very famous clients, as a matter
of fact. Tiffany Blume, who'd been the latest femme
fatale on a new series called Lotus Pointe.

It wasn't as if my mother hadn't seen it
coming. My father was forever working late, and then
working weekends. On one of those weekends when
he was supposed to be negotiating a multi-movie
contract deal in New York City, one of the gossip
rags had shot photos of him shirtless, in swim trunks
walking along a stretch of beach in Cancun, hand in
hand with Ms. Blume.

That was all it took for Mama to pull up
stakes. She'd never liked California, let alone L.A.
She'd been born and raised in the South, an only child
herself, who had been doted on by loving parents.

So, once she came face-to-face with the reality
of what my father had been doing, her Southern pride
kicked in heavy duty.

She'd packed us up, made flight reservations
and we escaped back to Tennessee to live with my
grandparents until Mama could figure things out, or
so that had been the plan.

Mama never had figured things out.

My father hadn't really fought the divorce. I think that in and of itself was the thing that affected her the most. Despite my grandparents' stern warnings that Mama deserved half of everything, and that she'd be better served by replacing her devastation with white-hot anger, her stubborn pride wouldn't have it.

"I want nothing from that cheating bastard!" she screamed. "I just want to be done with him. I should've known better than to hitch my wagon to a sneaky, good-for-nothing, Yankee!"

And then I had to listen to my grandparents say over and over again about how they had tried to warn her; that they never had cared for Randall Evans; and the fact that he had moved us all out to California, the land of sin and depravity, had been the kiss of death for their marriage.

Of course Mama was looking elsewhere to lay the blame. "You shouldn't have made me go to that college," she'd sobbed. "Y'all knew I wanted to go to school around here, not clear up there in New York."

And then that led to even more arguing about how it wasn't their fault Mama had been taken with a fast-talking

Yankee and got herself knocked up at the end of her sophomore year.

I'd had to leave the room. I'd heard it all before, and to be truthful, I didn't appreciate the way they talked about Daddy. No matter what, he was still my father and I loved him. I hadn't particularly liked him at the moment, but I couldn't simply stop loving him after all.

Mama had never understood that. In fact, she made such a big deal out of my going to spend a month with him the summer I was fifteen that she begged me not to leave her again.

So, when the following summer had rolled around, I had no choice but to lie to him. I told him I didn't want to visit, because I had so many activities planned for the summer and asked if he would mind. He said he understood, but I knew that it had hurt him, and for that, I felt bad. But, I just couldn't stand to upset my mother like that again. Their divorce had cost me dearly. Maybe more than it cost them.

So much more.

I dressed in a pair of ratty jeans, and pulled a clean tee shirt from my dresser drawer, shrugging it on over my head. I took a glance at my face in the mirror. At least I'd gotten enough sleep so there weren't any dark circles under my eyes. I didn't use make-up unless I had to cover dark circles or bruises.

21

I ran a brush through my shoulder-length blonde hair, and then pulled it up into a messy ponytail. I located my sneakers under the bed and slipped them on.

Hopefully Mama was still sleeping it off, and I could leave the house without having to deal with the usual bullshit that came with her hangovers: cleaning up puke, helping her out of her soiled clothes and into clean ones, and tucking her in to her bed while listening to her rants.

I grabbed an apple out of the bowl on the kitchen counter, shrugged on my backpack, and headed down the hallway towards the front door.

That's when I saw her bare feet, sticking out from the arched doorway that led into the living room.

Crap.

So much for getting a clean break from the insanity. I dropped my backpack to the floor and tossed my apple on top of it.

"Come on, Mama. Let's get you into bed," I said, walking through the doorway of the living room and bending down to shake her.

But she didn't move; didn't make a peep. Her arms were sprawled out in front of her, palms down on the hardwood floor. I noticed a piece of the broken bottle near the fingertips of her right hand.

My eyes quickly moved to her other arm, where blood from her left wrist pooled around it.

"Oh my God! Mama!" I screamed, scooting over to grab her wrist to get a better look. She had gouged it good with the piece of glass. Dried blood was caked on the wound, and then I heard her moan. I jumped up and grabbed the phone, dialing 9-1-1.

"Oh Mama," I said with a sob, "what did you do? What the hell did you do?"

CHAPTER 3

Three Years Prior

July 3, 1993

Malibu, CA

"Don't tell me you're going to waste a perfectly good holiday weekend sitting out here painting some stupid cliffs, Tennessee," Seth said, coming up the steps to the back of our yard where I was perched on a stool, canvas and watercolors at my fingertips as I continued painting my landscape abstract.

I glanced over at him, seeing that he'd brought a beach towel, was wearing his bright red swim trunks, and was palming his Nerf football in one hand.

"I'm painting today," I answered, looking back out over the horizon.

"Yeah, well you painted yesterday, too. You're letting some prime swim time slip through your fingers. Those cliffs won't be going anywhere soon. Come on, let's swim."

I felt the color rise to my cheeks. Why couldn't Seth just let me be? I would much rather be swimming, but I couldn't for another couple of days. I'd just gotten my period for the first time. Mama had explained what I needed to do, and that swimming was off limits until it stopped.

This whole menstruation thing was going to be a drag. I could tell already that I wasn't going to like it one little bit.

"Are you sure that's what this is, Mama?" I'd asked when I saw blood. "I'm just fourteen, maybe I should get another opinion."

"Oh for heaven's sakes, Neilah Grace! Of course that's what it is. You ought to be thankful you haven't started before now. I was barely twelve when I got my first period."

And so I had resigned myself to the fact that, for the next thirty or forty years, this would be my monthly burden. It totally sucked during the summer though.

"I can't," I sputtered, dabbing my brush into the magenta paint.

"Why not?" Seth pressed, scrunching up his forehead.

"Because I just can't!" I snapped, flashing him a dirty look.

And in seconds, I saw the flash of comprehension as it flickered across his face. "Oh, ragging it, huh?"

"Do you really need to be so crude?" I replied, looking away from him feeling totally embarrassed.

"Hey, Tennessee, relax. I get it. So, we can do something else if you want. Hey, I could have Rita drive us to the Santa Monica Pier."

Rita was the Drake's full-time housekeeper.

"What for?"

"To hang out. Maybe drop a pole in the water. Ride the Ferris wheel. Whatever."

I stopped mid-stroke and gazed over at him. He had his crooked smile going which deepened his dimple even more.

It seemed like Seth had sprouted at least a foot taller since the previous summer. I glanced down at where he had one foot resting on the Nerf ball and noticed his legs were starting to get man hairy. And then, for some inexplicable reason, I quickly looked back up to where I caught him gazing at me with a half-smirk going on.

"Well," I replied slowly, "this picture is almost finished. I guess I could. But doesn't Rita have to stay with the kids?"

"Nope, Laura took them with her to the set today. Said she needed more bonding time with her 'baby girls,'" he finished, rolling his eyes.

Seth called his mother 'Laura,' which I found very strange, but then, people did a lot of things differently in California I'd come to realize. He also called his dad 'Kent.' That's just how he was with his folks I guess.

"Okay," I relented. "I'll meet you over at your place in about fifteen minutes. You aren't wearing your swim trunks to the pier, are you?"

He cocked a brow. "Why not? It's Cali. It's all good."

"Whatever," I mumbled, gathering up my stuff. "See you in a bit."

And we'd actually had a blast at the pier. Seth had brought some of his fishing gear and actually taught me how to stick the bait on the hook so that we could fish off the end of the pier.

It was just us with a bunch of old guys who chewed tobacco and spit the juice out over the side of the railing with enviable precision. Their skin worn and weathered, as if they'd spent hundreds of hours of their lives fishing, just like they were doing that afternoon.

"This isn't half bad," I commented to him, as I'd felt a pull on my line. "Hey, I think I caught one!"

He'd immediately dropped his pole to come help me, instructing me how to reel in my catch, which, as it turned out, was an old black leather boot.

"Aww, that's a bummer," he consoled, "But you never know what you might pull out of the ocean I guess."

Later, we'd ridden the Ferris wheel about four times, got some ice cream, and then walked over to where some street musicians were trying to lure a totally fake snake out of a big, black urn with their flutes. I walked over and stuck a dollar bill in their glass jar.

"What'd you do that for?" Seth asked. "That's all fake, you know."

"I know," I replied, "but still, I was entertained so why not? I believe in supporting the arts, which includes musicians, Seth."

He rolled his eyes, and shook his head. "I don't consider that crap music *or* art. You're kind of weird, Neely."

"Yeah?"

"Yeah."

"Well, I reckon that's because I'm artsy. At least that's what my daddy says."

Seth studied me quietly for a moment as if he was considering what I'd just said. "Yeah. I guess you are at that. But you're okay anyway," he finally said. "Come on, let's go put our feet in the sand."

And, for the rest of that afternoon, we made wet sand pictures with our toes. Mine were so much better than Seth's even though he wouldn't admit it.

To make up for it, I pretended I couldn't grasp the knack of skipping stones on the lagoon that was on the other side of the beach. Seth patiently explained what I was doing wrong; and that it was all in the wrist snap at just the right time if I wanted to achieve multiple skips, but I just never seemed to manage it.

When Rita dropped me off at home later, Mama gave me what for because I hadn't taken my sunscreen with me. She made me stay inside for the rest of the afternoon, but that was okay, because I'd decided to work with my charcoals in my room. I loved sketching and shading with them.

By suppertime, I had a fairly good sketch of Seth standing against the rail of the Santa Monica Pier, with his fishing pole over the side and his ball cap on backwards. I pinned it to my bedroom wall that had been paneled in cork board from floor to ceiling.

It was where I displayed all of my exceptional work.

CHAPTER 4

Present Day

    I paced back and forth outside the double doors that led to the ER. I'd been told to stay put after the paramedics had wheeled Mama in there, her face covered with an oxygen mask, and her left wrist wrapped in layers of gauze. It seemed like it had been hours, but the clock on the wall said it was more like thirty minutes since she'd gone in there.

    I finally collapsed down on one of the chairs that lined the hallway outside of the emergency room. I buried my face in my hands. I needed to call someone. I didn't want to be here by myself in case…well, in case the news was bad. The medics hadn't told me anything. I'd had to ride up front with the driver who just kept telling me to stay calm.

But I had been calm. Almost too calm. At first, it was if I was watching it all unfold from someone else's eyes, not my own. I'd made the call, given the address, and described Mama's injury in a very calm manner.

The 9-1-1 operator had been really nice, telling me to find something clean to wrap around my mother's wrist, which I had done.

Before I knew it, I heard the screaming of the sirens down our street. The police had come too because they had to take a statement. I told them everything I knew up to the point of finding her there on the floor this morning before I left for school.

They'd asked me if I needed to call someone before we even left the house for the hospital. I had stared at them blankly. "There's really nobody to call," I explained. "I'm all she has."

"I meant for you," the officer had clarified.

"She's all I have," I responded before walking out the door behind the paramedics who'd placed Mama on a gurney.

But sitting here now, I knew that wasn't altogether true. I still had my father even though we hadn't talked to one another in ages.

And I still had my grandmother.

My grandfather had died last year, and when Mama and I had gone to the funeral home, it had been the first time we'd all seen each other in nearly a year.

Grandma hadn't approved of Mama's lifestyle, and made no bones about it even there that day.

"You smell of booze," she said after Mama had pulled her into a hug. "Drinking already and it's not even noon."

She'd pulled away from Mama and reached for me. "Neilah Grace," she said with a sigh, "why'd you let her drink before coming here to mourn her daddy?"

It took me a moment or two, but when I realized she actually wanted an answer to that, I was dumbfounded. I simply stared at her wrinkled face and wondered when I'd become the parent and Mama the child.

Mama proceeded to show herself once the minister began the prayers. She cried and sobbed, and dropped down to her knees in front of Grandpa's casket, clawing at it and asking "Why, Daddy, why?"

I had no choice but to intervene, going over to where she was and whispering to her to please get up and not make a scene.

"He's my daddy!" she had wailed, "I'll make a damn scene if I want to, Neilah Grace!"

Finally, the minister came to my rescue. He bent down and talked softly to Mama, telling her that her father was home with the Lord now and wouldn't want her grieving like that for him. She'd finally nodded and allowed him to help her back up to her feet, where she got a fit of hiccups that lasted throughout the prayers.

At the cemetery, there'd been more of the same and my grandmother had finally broken down as well, sobbing into her black lace handkerchief.

Afterward, Mama and I had stayed a bit so that she could say her final goodbyes. I had thought about my father. I hadn't seen him since the summer before. But it seemed longer than that. Much longer.

I heard the swish of the double doors leading from the ER, and a man with a starched white coat, and turquoise-colored scrub pants looked around. "Who's here for Nina Evans?"

"I am," I said, standing up. "I'm Neely. I'm her daughter."

"Dr. Reynolds," he said, holding his hand out for me to shake. He sized me up for a moment, probably trying to figure out how old I was and then he lowered his head and sifted through a couple of papers that were attached to the clipboard he held. "She's lost a lot of blood, but thankfully, she didn't hit an artery. I've stitched up the cut, and given her something for the pain. We need to keep her seventy-two hours for observation."

"Observation?" I asked.

He cleared his throat as if he was uncomfortable continuing the conversation with me. "Well, Neely," he began slowly, trying to select the least offensive words I imagined, "there's the matter of her injuring herself--"

"You mean trying to commit suicide?"

He nodded. "Yes, well, by state law, these attempts, when brought to the attention of medical practitioners and law enforcement, must be handled per the legal statute--"

I interrupted him. "Only seventy-two hours?"

He stopped mid-sentence and looked at me, clearly puzzled by what I'd just said.

"Doctor," I continued, "my mama tries to commit suicide every damn day of the week. Maybe not with a piece of cut glass, but with something nearly as lethal. She's a raging alcoholic."

He was still watching me, totally befuddled, if I was reading his expression correctly.

"She goes on benders for days, sometimes weeks at a time," I said, annunciating my words for clarity. "Her cutting herself? Well, that's just her way of trying to speed up the process since the alcohol is taking its good old time, I guess."

Dr. Reynolds looked shocked, but as I stood there staring back, I double-dog dared him to blame me for any of it.

"So, what you're saying is that you feel she needs longer term treatment?"

"Bingo," I replied. "She needs to dry out and talk to a shrink. Now, can you or can you not make that happen what with these legal statutes and all?"

Again, he cleared his throat. I was pretty sure I'd thrown the good doctor a curve ball. But this was my chance to make something happen. And Mama's chance to survive.

"How old are you, Neely?"

There it was. I wasn't surprised. I knew that question was coming.

"Seventeen."

"Ah. I see. Let me ask you this, is there any next-of-kin of your mother's that might agree to sign on as her legal guardian?"

I contemplated his words, wondering if, in fact, Grandma would step up to the plate on this one. "My grandmother...my Mama's mother is all there is. They don't get along. I'm just not sure..."

"Listen, Neely," the doctor said gently, "it's her best chance for recovery."

"I'll make the call," I replied solemnly. "All she can say is no, I guess."

I phoned Grandma and explained the situation. I was surprised when she started crying. I guess I'd half-expected her to say it was my problem now, but she didn't. She actually broke down.

"Of course, Neely. I'll be there right away, honey. I...I just don't know what's wrong with me that I didn't see this for what it was. Please forgive me."

"It's not for me to forgive, Grandma."

I hung up the phone and turned around to see Dr. Reynolds studying me thoughtfully. "She's on her way," I said. "She'll sign the papers to commit Mama for treatment."

"That's good," he said. "What about you?"

I gazed up at him, confused. "I don't think I'm ready just yet for that."

He smiled, "No, I meant who's going to be looking after you, Neely?"

I shrugged. "I've pretty much been looking out for myself since we moved back."

"I also have a legal responsibility to report minors who are left without care once your mother is taken in for treatment. That's all I meant. If you're not eighteen yet, I have to notify the Department of Human Services to intervene."

"No," I snapped, "there's no need for that. I have my father. He's in California, but he'll take me. I'm sure of it."

He nodded. "Good. You'll need to contact him and he'll need to contact social services to authorize assuming legal custody of you. I'm sure it can be handled by phone and fax, but it has to be approved by the court. Until then, I suggest you stay with your grandmother."

"Got it," I replied, getting ready to place that call to my father. The sooner the better. I wasn't up to having to put my grandmother back together. It was just too much. I wanted my old life back, and I wasn't too proud to admit it.

I prayed my father would want me as much as I wanted and needed to be there.

CHAPTER 5

Two and a Half Years Prior

Malibu, CA

Thanksgiving 1993

"I don't know why your father couldn't put off this meeting in New York," my mother said, leaning against the kitchen counter and sucking down her third--or was it her fourth--martini?

"Mama, something smells like it's burning," I remarked, walking past her where the double decker built-in ovens were located against the wall. Both lights were illuminated, and I bent down to peer into the bottom oven.

"Oh, Mama," I said, quickly grabbing a couple of the potholders from the counter and opening the oven door. "The turkey is burnt to a crisp!. See here?"

She glanced over at the pan as I set it on the counter and then started giggling. "Oops," she said, covering her mouth with her hand, "I think I' must've mixed them up. The turkey should have been roasting at 325. The other stuff at 425. Why that bird's been in there for five hours." And then her giggles segued into a fit of pure, maniacal laughter.

I reached up and turned both ovens off. "Never mind, Mama. I'm not in the mood for Thanksgiving anyway."

Her martini routine was getting out of hand. The more Daddy was gone, the more martinis she seemed to down. This was not like her, or at least it hadn't been except for the past several months.

"Listen," I said, taking her arm and pulling her out of the kitchen and toward our family room, "why don't you just relax. Watch some television. I'll fix us something to eat, okay?"

She waved me off. "Not hungry. Why don't you go on out and enjoy yourself, sugar. I'm fine. I'll just wait here until your daddy decides to call and check in with us. Go on now. Why don't you get your paints and make me a pretty picture?"

Clearly, she wanted me out of the house. I knew it was because of her need to drink without having me around to see just how much.

I grabbed my easel, canvas, and charcoals and headed out into the November sunshine. The one nice thing about Southern California was that inclement weather was a rare occurrence no matter what season.

I walked down to the beach, wearing a light jacket and one of Seth's ball caps he'd left by the pool during the summer. I suspected he'd done it on purpose.

He had a gazillion ball caps, and this one in particular was one of my favorites. It was the team cap for the Nashville Sounds, our minor league baseball team. I wasn't sure how he'd gotten hold of it, but he only wore it once and then left it by the pool so I called squatter's rights.

I'd pulled my ponytail through the hole in the back and, as I faced the water where a trickling of sailboats coasted on the water, I adjusted the bill to keep the direct sunlight out of my eyes.

I spread a blanket on the sand and started another seascape scene with sailboats. I had several already, but this one would focus more on the clouds overhead. A sign of stormy weather maybe?

I became lost in my sketching and shading, but that was fine. It was, after all, my sweet escape for the storm that was brewing. And I didn't mean out over the water.

No, the storm that had been brewing for months now with my parents. The tension between them was palpable. As much as I tried to disassociate myself from it, I knew it was impossible.

The sun was starting to move downward on the horizon when I heard the sound of footsteps coming up behind me. I wasn't startled. I knew it was Seth.

"Hey," he said, collapsing down next to me on the blanket, "Nice hat." His hand tugged at my ponytail playfully. "I thought maybe I'd find you here. Your mom's been looking for you. She called the house. Sounded kind of, I dunno, worried and upset."

"Did you talk to her?" I asked, setting my canvas down next to me.

"Yeah."

"So then tell me, Seth. Did she sound worried or upset? Because I doubt very much if she could've pulled them both off as drunk as she probably is by now."

He studied my face from where he sat across from me on the blanket, his legs pulled up in front of him, his wrists resting on his knees. "What's going on, Tennessee?"

I didn't want to tell him. And it wasn't because I didn't trust him or couldn't have used his take on the whole situation, because clearly I did and I could. It was that I was afraid I might break down and start bawling in front of him, and, well, that was just one thing I'd never done in front of Seth.

I surely didn't want to start now.

"Hey," he prodded, giving me a soft kick with his foot, "tell me, Neely. Maybe I can help."

I shook my head. "I can't," I squeaked.

"Why not?"

I looked down at my fingers, and started picking at my nails. "Because I'm afraid I might cry once I start talking."

He shifted closer and took the hand I was picking at and placed it in his. I hadn't realized how big Seth's hands were becoming. "So, what's wrong with that?" he asked softly.

His words pushed me even closer to the edge of the emotional cliff.

"I've…I've never cried in front of you. I'm not about to start now," I muttered, not looking at him.

"You know, Tennessee, we've known each other for what feels like forever. I guess I misjudged the depth of our friendship."

I glanced up at him, and narrowed my eyes just a bit. "Seth, do you think for right now, for this conversation, you might call me Neely?"

He gave me a pensive look, his mouth turned up a bit giving me a partial grin to take the edge off I suppose. "If I call you Neely, will you tell me what's going on?"

I nodded.

"Okay, *Neely*," he said softly, "please, tell me what's happened cause I'd really like to help if I could."

I kept my eyes from looking into his, because I knew that might prove to be a tipping point for me. "My mama is drinking all the time. My daddy's never home, and I think there's something very, very wrong with their marriage. I don't...I don't know how to act. I don't know how to fix it," I blurted out quickly. "And I wish we'd never moved to California because I think that's when things started to change," I finished.

Seth let out a long sigh, the hand that wasn't still holding mine, brushed the hair back off of his face. His kind and his very handsome face. When did he get so good-looking?

"Wow. Well, that's some pretty heavy stuff, I'll give you that. Can I think about it for a few minutes?"

I nodded. And we sat there in silence for several moments, he was still holding my hand, which kind of puzzled me, but I liked it.

"Got an idea," he said, standing up and pulling me up with him. "Laura is a great listener. And she's pretty good at problem solving, too. She's always helping my two sisters with something it seems like. Why don't you talk to her about the situation? I'm sure she can help."

I wasn't so sure anyone could help. But the thought of having another female to confide in appealed to me at the moment. "Well, is she busy getting dinner or anything?"

"Please," he said, chuckling. "Rita already fixed our Thanksgiving dinner. Hey, have you eaten?"

I shook my head. "Mama totally torched our turkey."

"Well then, you can grab something to eat at our place. Actually, you'll be doing me a favor."

"How's that?" I asked, crinkling my nose.

"Rita always makes way too much. We'll be having turkey in some way, shape, or form until Christmas. Come on."

And that was that.

He helped me gather my stuff, and then we trudged along the beach until reaching the wooden steps leading up to the back of his house.

I'd been in the Drake house plenty of times before. It always seemed as if I was walking into some prime time television show. Lots of activity and chatter---all of it good-natured. His younger sisters were a trip. Danielle was ten, and Christy was nine. They looked like twins of different heights.

Once inside, I could see that Seth hadn't exaggerated one bit about the size of the spread Rita had put out. The long cherrywood buffet in their formal dining room was full of platters, bowls, and baskets of everything one could possibly want on their dinner plate.

Turkey, dressing, mashed potatoes, gravy, cranberry sauce, macaroni salad, carrots, peas, sliced melon and strawberries, dinner rolls, tossed salad, and several different pies.

"Wow," was all I could say eyeing the spread.

"Go ahead, Neely. Grab a plate and help yourself. Lemme go find Laura."

I walked over to where a stack of clean china plates were stacked and grabbed one. I put some turkey and dressing on it, and some cranberry sauce.

As if Rita had built-in radar, she came bustling through the swinging door from the kitchen with a pitcher of ice water, and filled a clean glass with it, placing it in front of me on the table.

"Would you like me to warm that up for you, dear?" she asked, grabbing a silverware setting that was wrapped in a linen napkin from the stack on the hutch, and handing it to me.

"Uh, no m'am, I replied, "this is just fine. Thank you."

"Okay. Just give me a shout if you need anything else."

"Thank you," I said, unwrapping the silverware and grabbing the fork. I hadn't thought about just how hungry I was until Seth had mentioned food.

I had nearly cleared my plate when Seth returned, his mother, dressed impeccably in jeans and a blouse that somehow she made look kind of glamorous. She was so pretty. Her make-up and nails were always perfect. When I'd commented on that once to Seth, he had just shrugged saying it was the nature of the business for her to look 'picture perfect.'

"You never can tell when paparazzi will jump out and snap a picture," he explained.

"Papa--what?" I asked.

He laughed. "You don't know anything about show business, do you Tennessee?" he teased. "Pap-a-raz-zi," he repeated, slower this time. "They're photographers that follow celebrities around and try to catch a picture of them looking ugly or maybe doing stuff they shouldn't be doing."

I'd considered what he said for a moment or two, and finally, "Why?" I asked.

"Because they can sell the pictures to a tabloid and make good money, that's why."

"Are you talking about those newspapers they sell in the checkout line at the grocery stores?"

"Yep. Those are tabloids."

"Mama says they're trashy. And selling pictures? Well, that sounds kind of shady," I'd remarked.

"Welcome to Hollywood, Neely," he had replied.

"Well, hi there, Neely," Laura Drake greeted with a smile, taking the chair next to me.

"Hi, Mrs. Drake," I replied, swallowing a mouthful.

"Please, call me Laura," she said, "I feel like we've known you forever."

"Okay…Laura," I said.

She studied me for a moment, trying to select her words. "Seth told you about your mother calling here looking for you, didn't he?"

"Yes, m'am--Laura," I corrected. "Yes, he told me."

"Do you think maybe you should give her a call to let her know you're over here with us?"

Yes, I should. No, I didn't want to. I wasn't sure how plastered she was going to be, and sometimes that caused her to get a little mean with me. "I guess."

"Before you do," she interrupted as I started to get up from the table, "Seth mentioned to me that you had some concerns about how your mother's been acting lately."

I nodded. "She's been upset all the time. And now she's drinking. A lot. I think she and my daddy are having problems. She doesn't discuss it with me, but I can tell."

Laura was chewing on her bottom lip, as if she were contemplating her response. She probably figured a fourteen-year-old needed to be handled with some delicacy. It was funny, but I'd started feeling much older than fourteen over the past few months.

"Honey, sometimes married couples go through things. I know that Kent and I have. I call them rough patches. It's just part of life, and part of being married, you see. Now, I know your father's been traveling quite a bit, so I imagine your mother feels some loneliness on that account. I'm sure once he's done with all his *traveling*, things will get back to normal again."

There was something about the way she had said traveling that told me it was something much more than just that. Maybe Laura knew more than what she was willing to tell, or maybe she was just looking for some reason to give me so I wouldn't be overly anxious about my parents. Either way, she was trying to ease the tension I'd been feeling lately.

Her hand brushed against my cheek, and her fingers tucked a stray lock of hair behind my ear. She was watching me, studying me for some reason. "You know, you are quite stunning Neely. You're growing into a very beautiful young woman. Have you thought about what you want to do after college?"

That question came out of left field. But then again, I figured Laura wanted to change the subject to something more appealing. "I love art," I replied. "I hope to study art and maybe work at a gallery or museum. Plenty of those around here."

"Now that is a great goal," she said, smiling. "You know, one of my very best friends is curator at the Museum of Contemporary Art in La Jolla. How about if I set something up over Christmas break so maybe you and Seth can get a private showing? Would you like that?"

I felt my eyes widen and a rush of enthusiasm envelope me at the prospect of being able to ramble around an art museum of that caliber, taking all the time I want to look at the paintings displayed there. I'd read about it in the Southern California Tourist Guide. It was a pretty big deal here.

"Oh my gosh, yes! I would love that! But, I doubt if Seth would be into it," I finished, giving a slight laugh. "He thinks art is lame."

"Seth Michael," his mother admonished, looking over at where he was digging into one of the pies on the buffet. "You did not tell this girl art was lame, did you?"

He chuckled, shoving the corner of the slice of pie he held in his hand into his mouth and nodded. He chewed for a moment, and then cleared his throat. "You know Kent always says artists are starving."

"Oh nonsense," she remarked, waving her hand at him dismissively. "That's just an old saying. Art is forever. And it's passionate and compelling. I think a trip to the museum is just what you need to educate yourself on art appreciation."

He gave his mother a frown. "If you insist," he grumbled, as if he was truly irritated at the thought.

But I knew Seth. And I knew that he'd enjoy it almost as much as me because…well, because we were just that type of friends to one another. We did stuff other kids our age thought was lame or boring, but we always managed to have fun together.

"Well, I'll give Mama a call," I said, going into the kitchen where they had a wall phone. It rang a total of seventeen times before Mama picked up.

"Randy?" she asked, her voice a mixture of sleep and desperation.

"No, Mama. It's me," I said, twisting the phone cord around my fingers. "I'm over here at

Seth's house. They gave me something to eat. They've got plenty of food here. I'm sure I could make a plate up for you. Are you hungry?"

All I could hear was pathetic weeping from the other end. "I thought it was your daddy," she said, sobbing. "He never did call today like he said he would. He doesn't give a god-damned about us anymore, Neilah Grace!"

"Mama---" I started, but she didn't let me continue.

"I don't want any food. I want you home here with me. Right now, you hear me?"

"Yes," I replied.

"You can sit here with me and see just what kind of pain your daddy has caused me taking up with…with that *whore!*" she screamed. The phone went dead. I wasn't sure whether she'd hung up or pulled the phone cord out of the wall with as upset as she was at the moment.

I placed the receiver back on the cradle and turned to go back when I saw Seth standing in the doorway. "Everything okay?" he asked.

"Mama wants me home," I said quietly. I didn't tell him the rest because, to be honest, I had no idea what Mama had been talking about. She didn't always make a lot of sense after she'd had a few drinks.

"It's dark out. I'll walk you," he offered. "Laura is making up a plate for you to take home."

I nodded. And picked up the blanket and backpack with my art stuff in it, and strapped it on. Laura came bustling into the kitchen with a plate wrapped in foil.

"Here you go, sweetie. Try and get your mother to eat something, okay? And feel free to call me anytime, even if you just need to talk."

"I will," I said. "Thank you, Laura."

"You come back anytime, Neely."

The night was clear, the stars were twinkling above and the clouds had moved on as Seth and I made our way along the pavement out front to my house just down the road. We walked quietly.

I wasn't sure why he was so quiet, but I knew why I was. I was flat out dreading walking through my front door. I didn't know what to expect from the way Mama had acted today. She wasn't usually this crazy.

"What's wrong?" Seth asked, nudging me with his elbow as he walked beside me.

"Just kinda dreading going home. And I hate that I feel this way."

And then he did something so totally out of character, it nearly took my breath away. He slung his arm around my shoulders and just kept walking, as if this was a perfectly normal thing for us to do. I wasn't sure how I should react to it.

It wasn't creepy or anything. In fact, it was kind of nice. I felt protected and, at the same time, I felt like he understood.

We reached my front porch, and instead of Seth dropping his arm, he pulled me around so that our chests were just inches apart. I could feel the warmth from his body, and his breath caressed my cheeks. Before I had a chance to wonder just what the hell he was doing, I felt his lips on mine.

I balled my fists up at my side and was ready to plant them firmly on his chest when suddenly I didn't want to. I wanted his lips on mine. I liked the feel of them as they softly worked mine, tentatively and then a bit more urgently.

I raised my arms, and curled my fingers around his neck as I pressed myself into him a bit more.

Finally, he pulled back. We both caught our breath and I was feeling kind of dizzy. I figured it was because my head being tilted up while we kissed, might've slowed the blood flow to my brain a bit. Even my legs felt wobbly. I took a step back, staring at him.

What was I supposed to do or say now? I was so clueless with things like hugging, holding hands, or kissing. So I did what came natural. "Why did you do that?" I asked, wiping my mouth with the back of my hand.

He shrugged and flashed me a crooked grin. "Cause I felt like it, I guess. Not bad. Not bad at all. See you tomorrow, Neely," he said, backing off the porch, still grinning like a fool.

"Ask next time!" I called out after him, but he never responded or even looked back as he jogged back down the road.

I watched as he disappeared into the darkness, and it felt like butterflies were dancing in my tummy. For a second, I wondered if it was a weird type of menstrual cramping since my period was due any day. But I quickly realized it was a pleasant feeling unlike the former.

And then I smiled before walking into hell.

CHAPTER 6

Present Day

My dad popped the lid on the trunk of his rental car, and hoisted my suitcases into it, having to do some arranging to fit them all inside. It wasn't that I had a lot of clothes, I mean, I had enough, but I'd packed a lot of Mama's stuff, too. After all, I wasn't sure how long it would be before the landlord evicted us, and once Mama was released from the sanitarium she'd need them.

He slid into the driver's side and fastened his seatbelt, glancing over at me with a warm smile. "I know these aren't the best of circumstances, Neely, but it's good to see you again. How long has it been?"

"Two years, I guess. The last time I was at your house it was the summer I was fifteen."

"Hey, no more of this 'your house,' it's still *our* home, sweetie. It always will be. You know that."

I nodded, even though I didn't believe that. It hadn't felt like home to me since that Christmas when I was fourteen. When everything had hit the fan between Mama and Daddy. When Tiffany Blume had stolen my father's heart away from us.

"Is she still with you?" I asked. After all, it had been a couple of years. The chances were good that Ms. Blume had moved on to someone else's husband.

"*She* is Tiffany," he replied, pulling away from the curb in front of our house, "and yes, we got married a few months ago. I know she's not your favorite person, but Neely, I hope you'll at least be civil to her now that we'll all be in the same house together. You can't continue to blame her for what happened between your mother and me."

I glanced out the window, watching the familiar neighborhood I once called mine disappear from view. "I know that," I replied. "The blame is half yours too, Daddy."

"Look, Neely," he said with a sigh, steering the car onto the interstate, "I know, at your age, you probably see things in black and white, but life is more complicated than that, honey. Relationships are like, well, kind of like some of your abstract paintings. Blended shades and hues of colors, curves, softness, hardness, light, and dark."

"Yeah, I get it," I remarked, not wanting to hear anymore of his analogy using my artwork. "But it doesn't make it any easier for me."

"I know, and I'm truly sorry for that. But we fell in love, Neely. It just happened."

"You fell in love with Mama, too. Remember?"

I could see his hands grip the steering wheel a bit tighter. He didn't want to have this conversation, but he was the one that opened the door for it.

"Of course I did. But things change sometimes. What you want at twenty-five isn't always what you want at thirty-five. People sometimes outgrow one another. Their dreams and aspirations take different directions."

"Mama's never did," I replied. "She always wanted us to be a family. I thought that's what you wanted too."

He sighed, one hand left the steering wheel to run a hand through his hair. I could tell he was using something to cover the gray he used to have around his temples.

"And aren't you afraid the same thing might happen with Tiffany?" I pressed. "She's younger than you. How do you know she might decide what she wanted at twenty-five isn't what she wants at thirty-five?"

"I guess that's a risk I was willing to take, Neely. Can we please not argue about this? We've been through it all before the last time you visited."

Of course we had. I remembered. But things were different then. I'd had Seth to comfort me; to hold me, and to tell me that everything would work out for the best. He'd promised that, no matter what, he'd always be a constant in my life regardless of the distance.

"Sure. Let's drop it. I'll be civil to Tiffany. You don't have to worry about that. I appreciate the fact you agreed to take me in."

"Take you in? Dammit! You're my daughter. You could've come to live with me whenever you wanted. In fact, I'm upset you've had to go through all of this with your mother. You never said a word about her drinking."

"What could you have done about it?" I asked, turning my head to gaze over at him. I noticed his cheek was twitching. He was genuinely upset, that much I could see. It puzzled me a little bit. Did he really care about Mama?

"I could've done a whole hell of a lot had I known. My God, I would've gotten you out of that situation a lot sooner had you told me. You never answered one god damned letter I sent!"

And now it was my turn to get emotional. "What letters?"

"The letters I sent about once a month until I finally figured out you had no use for me. So, I stopped. I couldn't even get a phone number for you. So please, cut me some slack here, Neely."

I blinked several times as the ramifications of what he'd just said totally sunk in. "I never got any letters, Dad. And Mama said you had our phone number. She said you were just too busy with your own life now to care about calling me."

He was silent for a moment. "Oh, honey," he said, "my God, I had no idea that Nina was still so bitter. I am so, *so* sorry, Neely. If I'd known, there is no way I would have---"

"I know, Dad," I interrupted, not comfortable with how all of this was stirring up emotions I didn't want to deal with. I'd learned how to tuck them away into places I didn't ever have to visit if I didn't want to. "It's water under the bridge now. At least Mama is finally getting some help."

His hand left the steering wheel momentarily to lightly caress my cheek. "I want nothing more than for her to get better, and I truly mean that. And you? Well, I want you to figure out how to be a seventeen-year-old girl again. Not someone's caregiver, okay?"

I nodded. "I'll try my best. I need to finish my senior year. The semester just started. There won't be a problem in getting me enrolled at Malibu High will there? God, I hope my credits transfer without a problem."

"Hey, let's not worry about that, okay? I promise I'll do everything in my power to make sure it works out. Even if that means a private school or a tutor."

I rolled my eyes. "A tutor? I was on the honor roll at Bridgestone," I bragged.

"I don't doubt that a bit. Still wanting to pursue a degree in Art?"

"Not sure," I replied honestly. "I don't see things the way I used to see them."

CHAPTER 7

Christmas 1993

My dad watched as I opened the last of my presents. This one was from him alone. He said that he'd picked it out especially for me on his last business trip. He said the moment he saw it, he knew it would be perfect for me.

I tore the paper off and my breath caught in my throat when I saw it. It was a framed oil painting called 'Recognition' and it was a girl, looking in a mirror done in abstract, but I could tell the girl was me. "I don't understand." I started, puzzled at where he would've found a painting resembling me.

"The girl that painted this was blind, Neely. I saw her at an Art Fair when I was in New York. She was painting these abstracts while people described what they wanted, so I paid her to paint you. She did it all by my verbal description of you. I thought you might think that was kind of cool."

"Wow," I said, looking at every bit of detail, the colors, the intensity of her strokes, "this is so awesome. I can't believe a blind person did this, Daddy. I love it! Thank you!" I jumped up and wrapped my arms around him, giving him a huge hug.

"Had time to go to some art fair when you were there over Thanksgiving, Randy?" my mother asked. Her tone was petulant. "Maybe some time I could go along on one of your business trips. I'd love to do some sightseeing."

"We can talk about this later, Nina," he replied, still smiling.

It was so good to have him back home, at least for a couple of weeks anyway. After the disastrous Thanksgiving, it seemed to be just what Mama needed.

That evening, after Seth had walked me home, I hadn't been prepared for the scene I had walked into. Mama was passed out on the sofa, an empty liquor bottle dangling from her hand.

She'd cleaned out my father's closet and dresser drawers and must've busied herself all afternoon and evening by cutting each and every article of clothing into pieces. She'd even taken the time to cut out the crotches on each pair of his dress slacks, and then shape the cutouts into hearts.

I hadn't known what to do. I had no way of reaching my father on his business trip. And what good would that have done anyway? He was two thousand miles away. There was nothing he could've done about it.

I walked quietly over to where Mama was sprawled out on the sofa. I felt her neck for a pulse, and made sure I saw the rise and fall of her chest to make sure she was breathing.

And then I did what my instincts told me to do. I picked up the phone and called Laura Drake and asked her if she could please come down and help me with my mother. "Please. Don't say anything to Seth. Just come alone. I don't know what to do for my Mama."

For some reason, the thought of Seth coming down here along with his mother terrified me. I didn't want him to see her like this---to judge her, or worse yet, to pity her or me. This was a family matter. And since there was no family anywhere close, I had to take Laura up on her offer. And true to her word, she came alone and helped me get Mama up, showered, and filled up with as much coffee as we could get down her.

I'd been forever grateful to Laura that night. We hadn't spoken of it since. And blessedly, she hadn't mentioned it to Seth because he'd never made mention of it which would've been his style. By the time Daddy got home, Mama had gone shopping and presented him with a new wardrobe as an early Christmas present. He was never the wiser.

"So, I guess I did good, huh?" he asked, giving me a kiss on the top of my head, bringing me back to the present.

"I love it," I repeated, and then seeing Mama sitting stoically on the sofa, I continued. "You and Mama have given me the best Christmas ever. Thank you both so much."

"It was our pleasure," Mama said, taking a sip of wine. "Now, how about you pick up all the wrapping paper and bows and clear up the floor before dinner?"

"Sure thing," I said.

Later, after dinner, I told my parents I was going over to Seth's for a while. "I got him a Christmas present," I explained.

"Ah, sounds like there's a romance in bloom," my father teased.

"If you were home more often, Randy, you'd see for yourself how crazy that boy is for our girl," Mama snipped. "It's a bit worrisome keeping my eye on her by myself."

"Oh Mama," I said, grabbing my jacket off of the coat rack in the hall, "We're friends. Good friends. Don't embarrass me in front of Daddy."

"Yeah, Nina. You heard the girl. She's too young for any of that romance stuff, right Neely?"

I started to reply when Mama butt in.

"She'll be fifteen in January," she snapped. "Girls that age get knocked up around these parts."

"Later," I said, making a fast exit. I knew by now that Mama was ready to pick yet another fight with my father. It was no wonder he spent more and more time away on business.

Laura answered the door looking festive in a bright red velvet dress trimmed in forest green. "Merry Christmas, Neely!" she greeted. "Come on in. Seth's been pacing around waiting for you. He's in his room, you can go on up."

"Thanks, Laura," I replied, "and Merry Christmas to you too."

I went upstairs to Seth's room. The door was shut so I knocked.

"Yeah?" he called out.

"It's Santa!" I called back in a deep voice.

"'Bout damn time. Get in here."

Seth and I had grown closer since Thanksgiving. It wasn't anything that we worked on, it just sort've happened after that first kiss.

And that first kiss certainly hadn't been the last one. We perfected the art of kissing every chance we got. That is, when we were sure there were no prying eyes. My mother hadn't exaggerated one bit when she told my dad about keeping her eyes on us.

He was sitting cross legged on his bed, and had been listening to his stereo with his headset.

"How was your Christmas?" he asked.

I placed his gift on the desk while I tugged my jacket off, and tossed it on a chair in the corner. Then I picked it back up and placed it next to me as I took a seat on the bed beside him."It was good. You should see the oil painting my dad got me. It was actually painted by a blind girl. It's an abstract of me!"

"No shit? Sounds cool. I'll have to check it out. What else?"

I shrugged. "Oh, you know, the usual. Clothes, CDs, perfume, that kind of stuff."

"No jewelry?" he asked, cocking a brow devilishly.

"Nope. But then I didn't ask for any."

"Well, that doesn't seem right," he replied, pulling a wrapped box out from under his bed pillow. "Here. From me."

I tore off the paper and opened the small, velvet-covered box. I gasped when I saw the beautiful silver ring inside. It had two small diamonds on each side of a marquis-shaped pink stone. "It's beautiful, Seth," I breathed, taking it out of the box and placing it on my ring finger. "But garnet is my birthstone. It's red. I'm not sure what month pink is."

He was chuckling and rolling his eyes so I quickly shut up. "It's a pink diamond, Neely. This is a promise ring."

"A promise ring? Well, what is it I'm supposed to promise?" I asked, crinkling up my nose.

He reached over and took my hand in his larger one, gazing at the ring. "Promise me that I'm the only one you'll be kissing, how's that?"

When he said stuff like that to me my belly did somersaults. Right now they were in turbo mode. I felt my cheeks warm.

"I promise, Seth," I replied softly, my eyes locked with his.

"Let's seal it with a kiss then, shall we, Tennessee?"

His lips found mine, and his arms closed around my shoulders as we kissed deeply. My hands tangled in is hair and I felt tingly all over, just like I did with our first kiss. I wondered if it would always be that way.

I finally pulled back to admire my hand again. "I love silver, too. I have necklaces and earrings that will go perfectly with this."

"That's white gold, babe," he said. "And you can wear it with anything and everything. The point is, you're supposed to wear it all the time."

"Well, I know *that*," I mumbled, even though I hadn't known it at all. I admittedly was as green as a watermelon rind when it came to lovey-dovey stuff. But Seth sure knew a lot about romance things for a guy. I was impressed.

"So," he said, clearing his throat. "What's in the box there?"

"Oh," I laughed, "I got so caught up with my ring, I forgot to give you your present. I hope you love it as much as I love this," I finished softly.

I'd been working on it since Thanksgiving. I had wanted to give Seth something that was part of me. My painting was something that came from my heart and my soul. This particular piece, more than others. Because it was of him. It was painted with how he looked in my mind and in my dreams at night.

He tore off the Christmas paper and lifted the top off of the large coat box I'd found to put it in. I watched his face as he lifted the framed painting from the tissue paper I'd put around it.

I had been pleased with how it had turned out. The eyes captured the sparkle in his, and the smile was just a bit crooked, with his dimple showing. When Seth smiled, the sun had competition. His face was so handsome and his features so idyllic it was easy to understand why he would definitely have a future in modeling or show business if he so chose to follow that path. Which, up to this point, was still his plan.

"Oh Neely, damn," he murmured, "you did this?"

"Of course."

"It's like…well, it's like I sat and posed for it, but I know that's not possible. You did this from memory?"

"Yep. Sure did. I don't have to have you in front of me to remember how you look."

"Well, yeah. I get that. I picture you in my mind all the time. But to sit down and draw you, or even harder yet, to paint you with brush strokes, there's just no way I could ever do that! I love it."

"I'm glad," I replied. "I guess we each have our own talents. I know I could never do the whole performing arts thing like you're doing."

He got to his feet and took the picture with him. I watched as he removed the autographed picture of his hero, Wayne Gretzky from the wall over his bed, replacing it with my painting.

"I bet as soon as I leave you'll be putting Wayne back up there," I teased, giving him a playful swat on the behind.

He adjusted the painting so that it hung perfectly straight and then turned to me. "No I won't," he said solemnly. "This is so much better."

I felt myself blush, but he didn't stop staring at me.

"You're so damn pretty, Neilah Grace. No, that's inaccurate. You're so damn *beautiful*, you make my heart hurt."

"Sethhh," I whispered, drawing out his name, "you're embarrassing me here."

"I don't care. It needed to be said."

And then he pulled me up against him and we kissed for a long, long time.

On the way home later, I placed my fingers to my lips. They were chapped. I'd actually OD'd on kissing. We'd made out for like an hour. I knew I'd have to avoid Mama until I got to my room and put some ChapStick on them.

Tomorrow, Laura was taking us to the art museum in La Jolla just as she'd promised at Thanksgiving. And then on Friday, Seth would turn sixteen. She'd invited me over for dinner. I'd already been working on his birthday gift.

I'd started pottery lessons with my mother. We went every Wednesday evening. I'd kept it a secret from Seth because I wanted him to be totally surprised when I presented him with the special creation I'd been working on.

It had already been through the kiln twice. All that was left to do was to hand paint the details, which I was going to work on the next two evenings.

I sighed thinking just how lucky I was to have Seth.

A boyfriend.

Yes, that promise ring had changed our status, but truthfully, I knew our status had changed the night of that first beautiful kiss we'd shared.

CHAPTER 8

December 27, 1993

Mama had talked me into going to the mall with her to return some items Daddy had gotten her for Christmas. She claimed they weren't her style. Said they looked more like what some Hollywood slut might wear, not a Southern woman of refinement.

I'd kept my mouth shut on that one. Seemed like there was no pleasing Mama these days. She hadn't been drinking since Daddy returned, and that fact seemed to make her even growlier with everyone, including me.

So, the whole way to the mall, I jabbered about our trip to the art museum the day before. It had been so totally awesome, that I had a difficult time keeping me voice from raising every time I explained a different piece to her.

"I'm telling you , Mama, it was one of the best places I've ever been to. Even Seth enjoyed it and I never expected that in a million years! I could have stayed another day and not seen everything. Hey, how about you and me making a trip down there some time together? I just know you'd love it. They have pottery there, too. And lots of sculptures that I know you'd just love. Can we?"

She didn't answer.

"Mama, can we?"

"Can we what, darlin'?"

"Visit the art museum down in La Jolla. The one I went to yesterday with Laura and Seth."

"Oh, that's right. How was it? Did y'all have a good time there?"

I sighed. She hadn't heard a damn thing I'd said. God only knows where her mind was these days. "Yeah, Mama. It was real nice."

"That's good," she replied, turning onto the service road that led up to the mall. "You made sure to thank Mrs. Drake now, didn't you?"

"Yes, Mama. I thanked her."

"Good girl."

Thankfully, our time at the mall didn't take much time at all. It seemed all my mother wanted was to return her gifts for cash. Several thousand dollars worth of it as a matter of fact.

"Do you need anything before we get outta here, Neilah? she asked after the last item had been returned and she stuffed the money into her billfold. "I'm buying."

"Nope, I'm good. Where to now, home?"

She looked at her watch. "Damn, it's after four o'clock. Your daddy will be home from golfing by six. How about if we stop at Fry's on the way home and pick something already cooked at the deli?"

I shrugged. "Works for me."

Mama picked out some baked pork chops, Au Gratin potatoes, and three-bean salad at the deli. She grabbed a bottle of white wine from the cooler. "Anything you want for dessert?" she asked placing the items on the checkout counter.

"Can I grab one of those angel food cakes over there?" I asked, nodding towards the display table.

"Sure thing, baby girl. Hey, you watch this while I run over to frozen foods and grab some strawberries to go with it," she said, rushing past me. There was a customer ahead of us with a large order, so I knew she'd make it back in time.

I placed the angel food cake on the conveyor, and glanced around at the magazine racks lining the checkout waiting for Mama to get back as the conveyor moved forward just a bit.

It was then I caught a glimpse of a headline on the new edition of the "The Revealer." The words registered before the photo did. "Tiffany Blume is in full Bloom with her Attorney."

My eyes lowered to the photograph. It was the actress, wearing a skimpy thong bikini. The top of the swimsuit was mostly a cloth-covered underwire with two triangles of fabric that barely covered her nipples, as her breasts threatened to spill over the top. Two spaghetti straps led from the top and crossed over her chest tied in the back.

My eyes focused in on her *attorney*. It was my father, also in beach attire, his arm wrapped around her waist and her face was tilted up, looking at him with adoring eyes. The backdrop was a beach somewhere. The story beneath the picture merely described the candid shot being taken the day after Thanksgiving on the pristine beaches of Cancun.

Thanksgiving?

He was supposed to have been in New York, not Cancun. I froze, still staring at the picture when I felt it being pulled from my grasp.

"Oh my God!" my mother screeched. "I knew it! I just knew it! And he told me I was being ridiculous that lying son-of-a-bitch! Her calling here all times of the evening with some contract dispute! Him and his traveling here and there for the last six months on business! Yeah, right! Come on Neely, we're outta here!" she yelled, tossing a couple dollar bills at the cashier as she walked out with nothing but the tabloid in her hand.

"But what about our groceries?" I asked, not knowing what else to say.

"Leave them!" she shouted, "because we're leaving him. We've got some packing to do, girl! He can just come crawling back if he ever wants to set his eyes on you and me again!"

Mama drove like a maniac to get us home. Once there it was a whirlwind of activity. She was practically manic while dragging suitcases out, tossing clothes into them, and ordering me to do the same.

I was in shock.

Frozen with fear and panic. Not only did I have to try and digest the fact that my mother must've suspected this for some time now, but I had to deal with the fact that my father had found another woman to love.

I needed Seth. I didn't want to pack up my life and leave without thinking all of this through. Mama needed to talk to Daddy, to find out just what this was all about. Maybe there was an explanation for all of it. Maybe it was just like Seth had told me about those…what had he called them?

Oh yeah.

Paparazzi.

Photographers who followed celebrities around to catch them looking ugly or doing something they shouldn't be doing.

I wasn't going to leave like this. I needed my father to explain it all. To give us the truth first. To tell us that he loved someone else and didn't want to be a family anymore. And if that were the case, then I would go with Mama because I knew she would need me. But I wouldn't leave before talking to Seth.

In fact, right at this moment in time, he was the one I needed most.

Mama poked her head into my bedroom. "Get your butt in gear, Neilah Grace. I've made plane reservations and we need to scoot."

"No!" I screamed throwing a pair of my boots against the wall. "I am not going anywhere without talking to Daddy!"

"Oh yes you are, Missy! Don't give me any sass, we've got to get going!"

I was desperate. This had all come crashing down so fast I need time to think. "Okay, Mama," I said, in a tone that sounded as if I was resigned.

"Okay then. Be ready in ten minutes with everything you can fit in those suitcases. Your daddy will have to ship the rest of it out to us later."

She left the room and I crept over to the door and closed it silently, twisting the lock on the door knob.

I ran over to my bed, stood on it, and opened the window, pushing the screen out. I hoisted myself up and over the window ledge, dropping with a thud onto the shrubs that lined the side of the house. I quickly got my bearings and ran like hell out onto the road and down towards Seth's house, tears pouring from my eyes like a waterfall, but I didn't care.

There was a time for crying, and if this wasn't one of those times then I sure as heck didn't know what was.

I was out of breath by the time I reached the front door of the Drake home. I pushed the bell over and over again, afraid that if Mama discovered I wasn't in my room, she'd be down here lickety-split to drag me home.

Kent Drake answered the door, and as soon as he saw me, a look of alarm and concern crossed over his face. "Neely, what is it? What's happened?" he asked, opening the door wider so that I could come inside.

"I'm sor-sorry, Mr. Drake," I said, stumbling like an idiot over my words. "Can I please talk to Seth?"

"Sure you can, but first tell me if there's an emergency over at your house, honey."

I shook my head vehemently, "No, sir. Well, not in the way you're thinking anyway. I just need to talk to Seth before we leave for the airport."

"Go on upstairs. He's in his room."

I nodded and hurried past Mr. Drake. I knew by the question he asked that more than likely Laura had clued him in about my mother.

I didn't even bother knocking on Seth's door. I just pushed it open and barged in startling him. He was stretched on his bed, playing a video game.

"Hey, what's wrong?" he asked, quickly sitting up and tossing the controller on the bed. "Are you crying?"

I nodded not trusting myself to speak. He'd never seen me cry, and I was pretty sure I didn't look my best while doing so.

"Tell me, Neely. What's wrong?"

He was beside me now. All I could do was bury my face in his shoulder as I continued to sob. "It's my Mama. We're leaving. Going back to Tennessee."

He pulled back from me, his voice full of confusion and disbelief. "What? Why?"

I wiped my cheeks with the back of my hand. "It's those…papa-papar--what do you call them? The ones that take pictures and sell them?"

"Paparazzi?"

"Yeah. They took a picture of my father. We saw it in one of those magazines at the checkout. He was with some actress, on some beach. It was horrible!"

I dissolved into more tears, putting my hands over my face to hide my ugliness. "I just wanted to say good-bye," I sobbed into my fingers.

He wrapped his arms around me. "Shhh," he said in a soothing voice, "don't cry, Neely, please? I can't stand to see you upset. I'm sure your mother is just…well…pissed right now. She'll think it through and talk it out with your dad. You'll see."

Even Seth didn't sound convinced when he spoke those words, and he didn't know Mama the way I did. "No. She won't. I know her."

"Where's your dad?" he asked.

"Golfing. Supposedly. She wants to leave for the airport before he gets home. I snuck out. I'm supposed to be in my room packing my stuff. I climbed out the window," I admitted sheepishly.

"You did?"

"I couldn't leave without saying good-bye to you and letting you know what happened. And, well, if you want your promise ring back, I'll understand."

His hand cupped my chin and he tilted my face upward so that he could look into my eyes.

"Stop, Neely. I gave you that ring to keep. No matter what."

Just then Laura came into the room. "Honey, your mother is downstairs. She's waiting for you."

"Would you tell her I'll be right there?" I asked.

"Yeah. And Neely? I'm sorry, hun."

She left the room and I looked back up at Seth. "I'll write you when I get wherever it is we're going," I said, sniffling. "And I'll call you when we get a phone, I guess."

"Neely---" he started and then stopped. His face was flushed. Seth was upset. I'd never seen him like this before.

"I'm sorry I'm gonna miss your sixteenth birthday party. I had something back at the house for you. I'll leave it out on the back patio before we take off. You can come get it when you feel like it," I continued.

He was quiet now. Staring at me. Then looking upward so that I couldn't see his own tears starting to well up.

I stood there for a moment and then I wrapped a hand around his neck and pulled his face toward mine. Our lips met briefly for a kiss before another sob let loose from me. At least the tears had stopped for now.

"I love you, Seth Drake," I whispered before turning away from him. "And I'm gonna miss you like crazy."

I turned away from him and walked out of his room. I didn't dare look back, because if I had, I knew there was no way I could've held the flood of tears back any longer.

CHAPTER 9

July 10, 1994

Our house looked the same, but for some odd reason, it seemed foreign to me. It had only been seven months since we'd left, but it might as well have been seven *years* for how alien it all seemed to me now.

Same furniture; same drapes, same bedspread on my bed. I opened the closet door and empty hangers rocked back and forth on the rod. They looked lonely.

The oil abstract painted by the blind girl my father had given me for Christmas still hung on the wall over my bed. My mother had forbidden me from taking it, or having my father send it on to us in Tennessee.

"He was with that floozie when he bought that Neilah Grace! Remember? Lied about being on business in New York and took that whore to Cancun? She probably even touched it. I won't have it in my house, period!"

I hadn't argued the point any further. What was the use?

I quickly opened my suitcase to unpack. What I'd brought for the month wouldn't fill my closet, but it would sure make it look less lonely.

My father had a housekeeper now. Her name was Elizabeth, but she preferred to be called Betty. She wasn't full time like the Drake family's housekeeper, Rita.

Betty came in three days a week to do laundry, go to the market, clean, and cook meals for the week according to my father's menus.

Daddy had picked me up at the airport, taken me to lunch, and then dropped me at home where Betty was there to greet me and assist me in any way I required.

"Listen, Neely, I have to go back to the office. But I'll be home around seven for dinner. We can go out, or maybe grill something---whatever my little girl wants," he said, smiling. "It's so damn good to have you here, honey."

"It's good to be here. Don't worry about having to go back. Seth knew I was getting in today so we're going to hang out."

I saw a frown creep over my father's face. "Well, that boy is driving now," he said. "I don't want you going anywhere in that sports car he's got until I have a talk with him."

"Oh Daddy," I said, giving him an eye roll. "I'm fifteen and a half. I'm allowed to date, remember?"

"Since when?" he asked, his brow furrowing.

"Since now," I replied. "He's my *boyfriend*, remember? We've stayed in touch."

"I see," my father replied, still not pleased with the notion of me being on a date or in a car alone with my boyfriend. "Just stick around here for now, we'll discuss it later. The three of us." He kissed me on the cheek and left before I could protest any further.

The three of us?

The sun was starting to lower on the horizon. I raised my sunglasses up to look to my side. Seth was stretched out on his stomach, his head resting on his muscular arms, eyes closed. He was totally sleeping, which gave me ample opportunity to check him out without him knowing it.

I rolled to my side, propping my head on my hand so that I could assess my boyfriend thoroughly. I released a soft sigh.

Seven months had served him well, there was no doubt about that. He was several inches taller, and from what he said, he wasn't done yet. His arms and shoulders had somehow developed definition and muscles. In his phone calls to me, he'd said he had joined a gym to start working out.

His dark brown hair had lost that boyish, wispy look. It seemed thicker and coarser, and I could tell he'd started shaving, too. His sideburns were neatly trimmed short, and his eyebrows were a bit bushier than I'd recalled.

But the first thing I'd noticed when he'd scooped me up was his Adam's apple. Apparently it had made its appearance after he turned sixteen. And I'd missed it all I reflected sadly.

My eyes perused his tanned arms and flickered to where his left hand was exposed. He was wearing his class ring. He was going into his junior year of high school, but he wouldn't be returning to Malibu High this fall.

He'd written to me a few weeks back, letting me know that his mother had pulled some strings and he'd been accepted at The Southern California High School of the Performing Arts for his junior and senior years of high school. He was super excited about it, and as much as I wanted to share the excitement for him, I just couldn't. I wasn't sure why.

Maybe it was because he was able to pursue his dream, and I hadn't thought much about my dreams since the shit had hit the fan when my parents split.

As I continued to gaze at him, I realized that being here hadn't automatically made us pick up where we'd left off as if the seven months apart had never happened. I had felt tentative around him at first, almost shy.

Oh, we'd definitely kissed and held one another. But then he'd immediately taken my hand and announced we were going to the beach to hang out.

"Can I at least change into my swimming suit?" I'd asked, giggling nervously, "and grab a towel and sunscreen?"

"If you hurry," he replied, waggling his eyebrows up and down. So, we'd gone to the beach, hand in hand, and once we'd settled ourselves on the blanket, it hadn't taken more than a few seconds before Seth and I were making out like crazy, and suddenly the months apart seemed to disappear.

Studying him now while he slept he looked so darn perfect to me. He'd grown into this boy/man creature who was beautiful and talented, and I realized that just might be the reason I wasn't jumping for joy about his going on to pursue his dream of becoming an actor.

He was perfectly suited for it, there was no doubt about that, but he was still so young in my opinion. How was he so sure that getting his foot into that door of television or movies was what he wanted for the rest of his life?

It seemed to me that a lot of the younger television and movie stars ended up getting into drinking and drugs. At least that's what I saw on the tabloid covers at the grocery store many times.

I wondered if Seth did became famous, if he would still have time for me, or if he'd move on to some pretty actress or starlet. There was no shortage of them here.

So much had gone on in both his life and mine over the past several months that we had no way of knowing. It hadn't really gone the way I had hoped it would under the circumstances that had been forced on the both of us.

I thought back to that flight from California last December. Once Mama and I had gotten settled at my grandparents' home, I'd called him to let him know my new address and phone number.

After that, we'd call one another as often as possible. Then my grandparents had grumbled about their phone bills being sky high, so I wasn't permitted to call him anymore. I had to wait until he called me. So our phone chats went from every day to about three times a week.

Still, we had tried our best to make the best of the long distance. It was strange. Even when I lived up the road from

Seth, it wasn't as if we needed to see one another every day. But the fact we knew that we could was something that had been ripped away from us just as our relationship had risen to a new level. That part sucked.

I felt as if I'd been on the threshold of something so emotionally charged with the promise of it becoming some life-altering experience that I would forever cherish, and then suddenly, I was cheated out of it. Something I knew I was on the precipice of discovering; some unknown rite of passage I'd yet to experience, but was eager to taste. Well, all of that had hurt me terribly. I had ached for something I'd not yet fully known.

But the raw reality was that school, extra-curricular activities, and the three-hour time difference between us, had put a serious damper on our ability to communicate with one another as often as we would've liked.

Still, we had made a promise to write a letter to one another once a week, and we had both lived up to that pledge.

Seth had always typed his letters up on his mother's computer and mailed them to me in a manila envelope where he would include some sand from the beach, or tiny sea shells wrapped in tin foil. Once he'd included a cassette tape with music he said totally reminded him of me.

My heart and tummy had fluttered like a thousand butterflies had been let loose when I'd listened to his music choices for me.

The Right Kind of Love by Jeremy Jordan; *What is Love* by Haddaway; *Baby Come on Home* by Led Zeppelin; *Walking in My Shoes*, by Depeche Mode; *Take This Heart*, by Richard Marx; *When I Look Into Your Eyes*, by Firehouse; *When Can I See You*, by Baby Face.

From that point forward, I kept my Boom Box on my nightstand, and every night I played the cassette and fell asleep listening to the songs he'd recorded just for me.

"Hey, Tennessee," he said, his eyes now open, gazing up at me, shaking me back to the present. "What you doing, babe? Staring a hole through me?"

"Oh stop," I said, my foot kicking at his leg. "Just watching you sleep and thinking I guess."

He sat up, pulling his knees ups, and resting his arms across them. "Thinking about what?"

I shrugged, picking a piece of lint off of the blanket, my eyes not meeting his. I didn't really want to share what I'd been thinking, because, let's face it, some of it was kind of pitiful.

"Just that it seems kinda strange with us in some ways. I mean, you've changed in the last seven months. It's like you've grown up and I don't feel like I've kept up with you, that's all."

"Neely," he said, taking my hand into his larger one, "it's only been seven months, how much could've changed?"

I looked up at him. "You tell me, Seth. What has your life been like since I left? Who do you hang out with? How's school going? Do I still fit into your life even though I live thousands of miles away now?"

He was thoughtful for a moment. "Well, I've tried to keep you up to date as much as I can over the phone and with my letters, there's not much else to tell."

I knew what I wanted to say to him--what I needed to find out, but the truth was, I was chicken.

"Come on, Tennessee," he prodded me with his drop dead gorgeous smile, which made me wonder when I started thinking of him in those particular terms. "Tell me what's really on your mind."

"Okay," I said with a sigh, "you've gotten kind of...well, kind of handsome since I last saw you.

You're sixteen now which is supposed to be kind of a magic age..."

"Magic?" he asked, giving me a nudge this time with his foot, and an eye roll, "Define magic, please."

"Don't make fun of me, Seth Drake," I snapped, clearly irritated that for some reason it seemed as if he was getting cocky with me.

"Hey now," he replied quietly, "I wasn't, Neely. I'm just trying to get a handle on where your head's at right now. You're...I don't know, kind of being standoffish with me. All I'm trying to figure out here is why."

"I just told you why, Seth. I know it's not been that long, but you just seem older and different."

"Well, we're both a little older. You've grown too, babe. In all the right places, too," he whispered, scooting closer to me on the blanket.

I blushed at his reference to my chest expansion. It was true, I'd gone from a 'B' cup to a 'C' practically overnight it seemed. But it wasn't as if Seth had ever touched them. I hadn't missed the fact that his eyes strayed there several times while we'd been on the beach though.

"I'm not just talking about physical stuff, silly," I said, trying to get past the mention of my breasts. "What kind of people are your friends now? Do you…" I faltered for a moment, casting my eyes away from him, "do you ever go out on dates with girls?"

Seth scrambled up to a crouch beside me. "Is that what's bugging you?"

I nodded. "You turned sixteen the day after I left. You drive now. Even have your own car. You're starting your Junior year of high school. I know how social it gets when that happens. School dances, the prom. All those things are happening for you and I'm not here to share them with you."

"Yeah? Well think about the fact that I'm starting at a brand new school this fall where I will know zero people, huh? And what about you? You're going into your sophomore year at a school where at least you spent a couple of semesters at so you won't be totally clueless going in, right?"

"It's not just that, Seth," I persisted. "How can we maintain a long distance relationship? It's funny…when Daddy first moved us out here I hated it. As beautiful and golden as California was--and is, I ached for the rolling hills, lazy creeks, and dirt roads of Tennessee. I felt like I would never fit in here. But I did. And the reason I did was because of you."

"Me?"

I smiled and my eyes met his. "Yes, you. The nosy, asked-me-a-million questions boy that kept popping over to my house whenever he felt like it-- you. And I guess I thought I'd met a friend for life."

"You have, Neely. I promise. Nothing will ever change that between us. Yeah, I get that we're both too young to commit to anything serious. We both know that. But it doesn't mean we can't spend these next few weeks together. Hanging out. Having fun. And not dwelling on anything other than that. Because if we do, it will only bum the both of us out."

He was right, of course. Here I was, the first afternoon back and I was getting all weird and uptight on him. This was just the cards that had been played. I was fifteen and a half. My future, for the moment, was not in Southern California. It might never be. But I wasn't going to waste one more precious moment dwelling on that.

This was about the here and now. Living for this moment in time and enjoying the boy that had been my best friend for the past five years. Anything other than that wasn't in the cards, and I knew it. I could accept it because really, I didn't have any other choice now did I?

"Hey," I said jumping up, "come on! Let's go for a swim in the pool. Then Daddy said something about grilling out. Can you stay for dinner?"

Seth jumped up and pulled the blanket with him. "Now you're talking. And don't worry, Neely. I'll talk your old man into letting me drive you around in my car. We've got wheels this summer and we sure as hell are going to make the best of them."

CHAPTER 10

Present Day

I glanced around my bedroom, a feeling of déjà vu draped over me like a shroud. It had been two years since I'd done the same damn thing. The last time I'd been here. I had been fifteen (and a half). I smiled to myself. For some reason, that 'and a half' had seemed a big deal back then. Maybe because I was counting the days until I hit sixteen.

Sixteen. One of those special milestones.

Eighteen. The next milestone.

Twenty-one. The next special milestone after eighteen.

They each had their reasons for being special. Getting to drive, getting to vote, getting to drink legally.

Big fucking deal.

I'd gotten my driver's license. I'd even been drunk a couple of times with my girlfriends back home. And yes, I got how risky that was what with my mother's affliction and all, but I figured the odds were at least fifty percent in my favor that I didn't inherit that particular gene from her.

So here I was. Seventeen and in the same bedroom where I stood in two years ago and reflected in fifteen-year-old terms how my life had changed, but my room hadn't.

This time it was different.

My room had changed.

Completely.

There was nothing familiar here except for the oil painting that had hung over the bed. Now it was hanging on the opposite wall.

The walls were no longer a pale pink as they had been. They'd been repainted a soft cream, with a border of dark teal, maroon and ivory geometric patterns at the top of each wall where it met the stuccoed ceiling.

My double bed with the maple frame had been replaced with a queen size bed, with a wrought iron headboard. The duvet was a deep teal, and the mountain of throw pillows clustered at the head of the bed was in various shades of teal, maroon, and gold.

The room still smelled of fresh paint and new carpeting. I looked down at my feet. The new carpeting was thick champagne-colored plush. Each step I took, I felt myself sink into the rich luxury of it.

There was a new dresser and matching nightstands. Jewel toned tiffany glass lamps were placed on each one. My bed was in a different corner of the room.

My corkboard wall was gone. It didn't matter though. I'd taken every piece of artwork off of it when we'd left.

As far as I knew, it was all still boxed up in the cellar at our apartment. I hadn't thought about those paintings in forever. I hadn't painted anything in forever. Not since the summer and into the fall that I'd come back early from my visit with my father.

I glanced over and saw that the bedroom curtains had been replaced by ivory colored blinds. The room was dark with no sunlight coming through, so I quickly remedied that by twisting the wand to open the slats.

There. That was much better.

Mama had always said that sunshine was the cure for anyone's gloom. Funny, I thought, that sure as hell hadn't been her first choice in chasing away the blues, had it?

Is that what I was feeling standing here right now?

Was I feeling blue?

I wasn't sure why I would be. If anything, I should be overwhelmed with relief, gratitude, the intervention of the Almighty for saving my mother and, maybe, in the process, for saving me as well.

Just then there was a soft tap on the door. "Neely?" a feminine voice called out from the other side, "it's Tiff. May I come in?"

Of course it was *Tiff.* Who else would I have expected being that she was now my father's wife?

"Sure," I called out, grabbing one of my suitcases and tossing it up on the pristine duvet. The one she no doubt had selected when she decided to give my bedroom a complete facelift.

I turned back around to face her as she came through the door. "Hey, honey," she said, her voice carried a nervous lilt, which I found kind of fascinating. She was an actress after all, how difficult could it possibly be for her to play this role?

Her breath caught in her throat when she saw me. Had I been giving her the evil eye or something?

"I'm sorry, I mean hello, Neely. I just wanted to check in to see if you needed anything at all."

"No. I'm good. Thanks." I didn't turn away. She was studying me. Whether to read my mood or my mind, I wasn't quite sure, but I wasn't about to break eye contact. She was beautiful in a painted up, Hollywood glitz sort of way I suppose.

"You are so striking," she commented, walking closer as if to see if it was merely the lighting in the room that prompted her comment. "I haven't seen any recent pictures, but you are stunningly beautiful."

"Thanks," I murmured, wondering if I was supposed to return the compliment. Was this a new California thing? "I can't take credit for how I look though. It's just the way I turned out I guess."

"Well, you'd be a natural in the business," she replied, her index finger now tapping her cheek as if deep in thought. Planning my future? Setting a path for me?

No damn way.

"The business?" I asked, pretending not to know what she was getting at here.

"Hollywood. Films. Television. Modeling. My goodness, there are a plethora of opportunities for a young woman like yourself."

"No thanks," I deadpanned. "I've seen firsthand what that kind of career choice does to people."

It was a slap in her face, but that's okay, because it was supposed to be. If Tiffany Blume…sorry, Tiffany *Evans* thought she could win me over by remodeling my room and taking me under her wing so that she could mentor me into showbiz, she was plum out of luck.

"Look, Neely," she said, her hands now clasped together, "I know you're not here under the best of circumstances. And I know that you've got no reason in the world to like me or even allow me to be your friend. But I would like to at least try, wouldn't you?"

I dropped the tee shirt I'd been folding onto the bed and crossed my arms, locking my eyes with hers. "I promised my dad I'd be polite and civil, and I will. Beyond that Ms. Blume, you hold no sliver of interest for me. Now, if you don't mind, I'd like to finish unpacking here."

She visibly bristled, and a coldness swept over her face. "No problem. Dinner is at seven. Your father will be back around then. In fact, he's bringing you a surprise, so I hope you don't spoil that for him with an attitude."

She was at the doorway now, looking back over her shoulder at me. I stalked over to where she stood, my right hand bracing the edge of the door.

"Just as long as it's not a fucking puppy," I said, shutting the door slowly in her face.

∞

As it turned out, my surprise was a '96 Mustang. Convertible. Cherry Red.

"I--I don't know what to say, Dad. I mean, I love it. Can I take it out? Now?"

He chuckled, "Of course, Neely. That's why I got it. You're almost eighteen. You need your own ride living here in the boonies."

"Yeah, right," I said laughing, taking the keys he dangled in front of me. I dropped a kiss on his cheek. "Thank you, Daddy."

"You drive carefully, you hear? Tomorrow we'll have to get you a California driver's license."

"I will," I reply, starting the engine and revving it up. "And tomorrow we have to get me enrolled in classes, don't forget," I called out as I put the car in gear and headed out onto our road.

As I passed Seth's house, my eyes naturally gazed over at the circular drive in front of it. Three cars were parked along the drive. None of them his, unless of course, he'd changed vehicles in the last couple of years, which I suppose was a possibility.

I focused my eyes back on the road as I blew past their estate, my long hair blowing out as the wind whipped through it, giving me the first feeling of elation in a long, long time. It was invigorating. It was therapeutic. It was just what I needed to survive this part of my young life.

And I would survive. I knew that now. My time spent being my mother's keeper was done. It was over.

No more cleaning up vomit from wherever she happened to puke while she staggered around our apartment, trashed from the liquor and cursing everybody she deemed responsible for her current situation.

No more changing her wet sheets when she was too drunk to get up and use the bathroom; or listening to her rants about how things should've been instead of getting off her ass and taking ownership of her life, and mine, like a parent was supposed to do.

I loved Mama, I truly did. But I wasn't what she needed right now. I wasn't equipped any longer to see her through the drunken binges. Or the ranting and raving they brought, along with the fits of rage that sometimes had her swinging her fists my way because, damn it, I was a part of *him*.

I could forgive my father for what he'd done, because I knew he truly fell in love. But that didn't mean that I would ever warm up to Tiffany Blume, because yeah, I did not see that happening at all.

For now, my job was to finish school, and then continue on to college. I would never hang my hat on one man like my mama had done. I would support myself, and my lifestyle, whatever that happened to be, on my own.

I would never need anyone other than myself. If I loved someone, I would make damn sure that person was worthy of my love.

And if down the road it turned out that I wasn't enough for him, or he wasn't enough for me? Then so be it. I would move on and not look back and I would expect him to do the same.

I wanted no emotional chains binding me to someone I no longer wanted to be with, nor would I want to bind someone to me that wanted or needed to be somewhere else. What would be the point? Hadn't I already learned that lesson earlier?

I would never waste years of my life getting wasted like Mama had, still allowing herself to be tortured over something that just wasn't meant to be.

I knew that sounded judgmental, and I truly hoped like hell she could finally learn to cope. That through rehab and psychological counseling at the treatment center, she was getting the help she so desperately needed to heal. And to live the rest of her life not being miserable over something she couldn't change. She needed to let it go. Get over it. Go on with her life.

As for me?

I would never completely give my heart away. I may loan it out on occasion, as I saw fit, but it would always be mine to own and protect.

If I'd learned anything through all of this, it was that people need to accept the fact that life is what you make it. You define your future, as well as your successes or failures going forward. Life is what you make it. It's not what other people make for you.

No fucking way.

Not ever.

CHAPTER 11

July 24, 1994

I'd been at Daddy's for exactly two weeks and
I hadn't had a chance to talk to Laura yet, other than
to say 'hi' or 'bye' to her in passing. I'd been hanging
with Seth almost daily, but we were always going here
or there in his car, or when we were at his house, it
was only for him to grab his keys, or a jacket, or his
wallet.

I walked down the road toward their house. I
knew Seth had started his summer acting workshop at
the Pasadena Playhouse. It went from ten until four,
three days a week, which kind of sucked, but he was
really into it so I pretended to be happy for him. I
wished I had some of my painting stuff with me, but

there was no way I could've lugged all of that crap on an airplane.

I decided to take a walk down to Seth's. It was a little after three so I thought maybe I'd have some time to visit Laura for a bit before he rolled in. The fact I hadn't done that yet felt kind of rude.

Rita let me in, greeting me in her usual cheerful way. I asked if Laura was home, and she directed me out to the patio.

As I stepped from the cool house out onto the sunny patio, Laura looked up from where she was reading something at the table and smiled. "Well, it's about time you stopped over to visit with me, Neely," she said, motioning for me to take a seat next to her.

"I'm sorry, m'am," I said, sinking down into a chair. "I know I should've stopped by sooner."

"Oh Lord, you're back to the m'aming me. I certainly know why Seth refers to you as Tennessee," she finished, flashing me a warm smile.

I laughed with her, "Sorry--Laura," I corrected. "Am I interrupting you?"

"Not at all," she replied, shaking her head, "I absolutely love the interruption. I'm reading over a script and, to be honest, it stinks. I think I'll be telling my agent to take a hike if he continues sending over crap like this. Would you like some tea?" she asked, nodding toward the tray that had been placed on the table with tall frosted glasses and a pitcher of iced tea. Slices of lemon were floating inside.

"Sure, thanks," I replied, "I've got it." I filled a glass and took a sip. The tea here wasn't quite as sweet as what I was used to back home.

"So, how's your mother doing, Neely?" Laura asked as she took a sip of her tea.

I considered whether I really wanted to go there with Laura. The easiest thing to do would be to lie and get off the subject with a simple, "Oh, much, much better, thank you."

"She's not doing very well. We're moving out of my grandparents' home as soon as I get back. Mama isn't getting along with them very well."

"Oh? I'm sorry to hear that, honey. Is..."

I knew what she was going to ask, but for some reason she stopped herself. She probably thought it wasn't good breeding to inquire about Mama's drinking, but I had no issue with it.

"Yes, she's still drinking. That's the reason we're moving out of my grandparent's house. Going to another small town, far enough up the road that people won't be in Mama's business anymore. At least that's what she says."

Laura reached over, and her hand gently brushed a lock of hair from my face. "I know you've been through a lot this year, Neely. I can't imagine how tragic this all feels to you--at your young age to have your life torn apart the way it has been. Sometimes adults make mistakes. It's just a damn shame when it spills over onto their children."

I shrugged, not sure what to say because she was right. I felt like the victim in all of this drama. The victim of something I had nothing to do with.

"Have you forgiven your father yet?"

"What choice do I have? He's my father. I have to forgive him I guess. I don't have it in me to hate him."

"Well, honey, have you thought about living here with him?"

I nodded. "Yeah, I have. But, it's not an option. Mama would never allow it, for one thing. And even if Daddy went through the courts and won, well who would be there to look after Mama? I'm all she really has, you know?"

Laura gazed over at me thoughtfully. "You're such a beautiful person, Neely. You're just so young. I hate to see you in a situation like the one you're in. I know that Seth and you were...*are* close. It's just a shame what's happened."

"Thank you," I replied, taking a sip of my tea. Laura tapped her fingers against the tabletop, and I knew there was more she wanted to say. She was trying to figure out how to say it I suspected.

"You know, Neely, Seth's going to a new school in the fall."

"Performing Arts, I know," I replied, "He doesn't talk about anything else most of the time."

She laughed good-naturedly. "I can only imagine. He's had that dream for as long as I can remember. I think it all started when he was just a toddler. I would sometimes take him to the set with me. He learned the business literally at my knee, as they say. I guess he's as passionate about his craft as you are about your painting. Both so talented. This is such a great opportunity for him."

"I know it is, Laura. I'm really happy for him."

121

She sighed, and leaned closer. "I'm beating around the bush, aren't I? she asked.

"Yep. A little bit."

"Okay. Woman to woman then, because it seems like you've become one over the past seven months. You are incredibly pretty and well, I know Seth simply adores you, Neely. Trust me, I am not trying to pry into your personal business, but he is my son, my oldest and I can see where you two spend a lot of time together. Sometimes alone."

She cleared her throat, and downed a bit more of her iced tea. "I was young like you at one time. And my home life? Well, it wasn't a pretty one either. My parents fought constantly, and when they did, they fought dirty. I was the oldest, with two younger brothers. At times, I felt like I had to be the adult for them. It wasn't easy, and it wasn't a healthy situation. So, I guess what I'm saying is that in a way, I can empathize with what you've been going through."

"I appreciate that, Laura, but I'm not looking for anyone's pity, please. That makes me feel even worse."

"Oh no--no, honey. I'm sorry. I didn't mean it like that at all. You see, the point I'm trying to make--

and evidently, failing miserably at, is that at your young age you might be inclined to take a path to get out of the situation you're currently in with your family. An escape mechanism."

"An escape mechanism?" I asked, not following her at all.

"Well, I just want to make sure that you and Seth are being...responsible. And careful. You're both so young. You have so much living to do before--"

"You think we're having sex?"I asked, my voice louder than I intended. I was not only embarrassed, but I was kind of horrified that she'd be having this talk with me instead of her son.

She waved her hand dismissively. "I'm not here to drill or lecture you, honey. I just wanted you to know that I understand, because believe it or not, I was once where you are now, and I was tempted to find some way out."

Now I got it. "Oh, so you're worried that since my parents have split, and I've been taken away from my dad--and my boyfriend, I might try to trap him with getting pregnant?"

Her face blushed crimson telling me I'd hit the nail right on the head. "No-no, not at all. I know you'd never do that on purpose, honey. I'm just saying that, with teens, emotions and hormones can run amuck. You'll get through this, Neely, because you're an intelligent, talented girl that possesses a lot of strength for one so young. All I'm saying is that if you should find yourself, well, in a sexual situation, that you make sure precautions are taken so you don't get into any trouble," her voice trailed off.

In trouble?

Did people still used that phrase? Laura wasn't that old, was she?

I won't lie, what she'd just said to me I found a bit screwed up. I wasn't desperate. Yeah, my situation pretty much sucked, but I wasn't trash and I never would be. Then again, I wasn't about to lash out at Seth's mother. Someone who, up until now, had always been sweet and supportive towards me.

"Laura," I said, my eyes meeting hers, "you don't have to worry. Seth and me? Well, we haven't crossed that bridge. I'm only fifteen. I care about Seth. I wouldn't do anything to screw up his life, no matter how bad mine is right now."

I felt the tears welling up in my eyes. I was hurt that she thought I was that desperate, or that sneaky that I'd do something like that on purpose.

"Oh dear," she said, her teeth tugging at her bottom lip. "I didn't mean to upset you, honey. I'm so sorry. Please...please don't cry." She reached over and rubbed my shoulder with her hand. "If it makes you feel any better, I had this talk with Seth."

It did make me feel a little better, but also way curious.

"You did? What'd he say?" I asked.

"Basically, the same thing you said, but I know how that goes. Sometimes you just kind of get caught up in the moment. Trust me. Seth was Kent's and my little 'surprise.'"

"He was?" I asked, my eyes widening. "You mean...he was an *accident?*"

"Well, I prefer to say a surprise, but that's not really accurate when you don't bother with a condom," she replied with a laugh. "I mean, I don't regret him for a minute. It worked out very well for all concerned, but sometimes it doesn't, honey. That's all I'm trying to say here."

"I understand, Laura. And please, don't worry. I'm not ready to take that step anyway. And Seth has never pressured me or anything," I finished, feeling my cheeks warm because that part was an out-and-out lie, but I wasn't going to rat out my boyfriend.

The truth was, over the past few weeks, Seth and I had gotten into some pretty heavy-duty petting. (I hated that word, but really, there wasn't any other word to use.) I was the one responsible each and every time to put a stop to going any further, and he wasn't happy about it.

"Come on, Neely." he rasped, his hands moving over my breasts, his breathing coming harder and faster as his lips traced a path down my throat to my chest. "You know it's what we both want."

"Seth," I pleaded, "I think we're too young for this. It'll change everything between us."

"I know," he replied, his other hand slipping down beneath the fabric of my shorts, "it'll make everything so much better. You'll officially be mine and I'll be yours."

His fingers now explored the most private parts of me; his tongue traced a nipple causing me to shiver with pleasure, and my resolve was quickly slipping away. I had only seconds to turn the situation around and return to safe ground. I had known that much. But did I want to?

My mind said 'yes' but my hungry body wasn't so sure I wanted any of this to stop. This was Seth. My Seth. My boyfriend. Wasn't this the type of thing that boyfriends were supposed to do? Wasn't it natural and human to desire one another in a sexual way?

I damned myself for not putting every doubt or reservation out of my fifteen-year-old mind and simply going with it, because that would have been the easiest thing to do. And it would prove my love for Seth, just as he wanted to prove his love for me.

But in my Neilah Grace Evans way that is not what I had done. The thought that Seth had actually never declared his love for me with words somehow nagged at me. Sure, his letters always ended with 'Love, S.,' but he'd never actually written 'I love you,' in them.

Oh, I had said it to him once. That day Mama had packed us up and was ready to strip me from his life. It had been the very last thing I'd said to him in fact. But I'd been waiting all this time, through letters and phone calls from him to hear it back, and I never had.

So, I had picked that moment in time, with Seth's hands and lips all over me, to use that one little detail to propel me to stop him from going any further.

"Stop it," I snapped, my hands snaked up between us and I managed to push his head away from me. "I'm just not ready for this."

He'd been pissed. For one of the first times ever, Seth had been pissed at me. "Fuck, Neely," he snarled, "how the hell am I supposed to deal with this?"

I wasn't exactly sure what 'this' meant. His horniness? My reluctance? Our long distance relationship?

We hadn't discussed it further. I'd put my top back on, he'd adjusted himself in his jeans, and then drove me home in silence.

That had been last night.

And today's talk with Laura sealed the deal. This wasn't going to work. No matter how much I cared for him, or how much he cared for me, this just couldn't work when I lived halfway across the country.

"Do you care if I go up to Seth's room?" I asked Laura as she started to skim through the dreaded script once again. Things had grown a bit uncomfortable I guess after our talk. "I left a couple of my CDs up there and wanted to get them."

"Sure honey, you go right ahead. He should be home in thirty or forty minutes. And Neely?"

I turned from where I now stood at the patio door.

"How about we keep our little talk just between us girls?" she asked, giving me a smile and a wink.

"Sure, Laura. No problem."

Up in Seth's room, I gazed around. The painting I'd done of him still hung over his bed. Just like he said, he hadn't put Wayne Gretzky back up there.

My eyes moved over to his desk. There was his birthday present from me. He'd gone over to our patio and picked it up like I'd told him to do.

It was a clay pot, in the shape of a heart. I'd fired it and then painted it in a colorburst glaze called Black Iris. It was mostly black, but had flecks of red and gold in it for a rich, masculine look. I'd etched our names inside the bowl.

'Seth + Neely = 4-Ever'

I fingered the etching gently, thinking how childish it seemed seven months later. Seth had placed it right next to his computer monitor. He'd just gotten one this summer. He would need it for school he said. He'd asked if I had one so that we could start emailing one another.

Sadly, I told him a computer was not in my immediate future. It wasn't that Daddy wouldn't have bought one for me if I asked, because I knew that he would have. But what good would that do? How would I get it back home? Besides, Mama probably wouldn't allow me to bring anything he bought me into the house anyway.

I sat down on Seth's bed, and picked up his bongo drums from the floor. My hands started a rhythmic tapping, going back and forth between the two, banging out some tune I'd heard him play before. He was actually pretty good on percussion.

I needed to stop beating around the bush here. I hadn't come up here to pick up anything of mine. Just the opposite. I'd come up here to leave something of Seth's.

I set the drum down, and scooted off the bed, going over to his desk. I picked up a pen and a sheet of paper out of his printer. I hesitated momentarily, searching my brain for the right words.

Were there any *right* words for this?

Seth,

Decided to go back to Tennessee early. Good luck with your new school. I hope everything goes well for you there! I think both of us are too young for promises.

Love,

Neely

I pulled the promise ring he'd given me from my finger and dropped it into the heart bowl I'd made for him, listening to it clatter against the glazed ceramic surface. I folded up the note and placed it on the top so he'd easily see it. And then placed it on his bed, so he wouldn't miss it.

I wiped a tear from my cheek, and took one last look around his room. I walked to the bedroom door, and my fingers rubbed against one of his hoodies that hung on the door knob. I lifted it up, and buried my face into the soft fleece. I allowed a couple of sobs to escape, while breathing in his scent one last time.

Laura was right. Everything she said to me was true. And she said it out of love for her son, and concern for the both of us, I'm sure.

We were both so young. Distance had separated us from exploring anything other than our own futures apart. The most we could ever be to one another were pleasant and happy memories of our youth.

I'd had more than four years of being Seth Drake's friend; and for seven and a half months of that, his girlfriend. He was my first boyfriend. He'd given me my first kiss. He was responsible for my knowing how love felt, however fleeting, it was, and awakened other physical feelings within me that someone else would eventually fulfill.

It wouldn't be Seth, and that fact saddened me, but I understood the practical part of all of this.

Laura was right.

She was so damn right.

Mama and Grandma were at the airport in Nashville waiting for me at the gate. As soon as I came through the door I saw them.

"Neilah Grace, over here!" Mama called out waving frantically. Her face was as happy as I'd seen it since before our family had imploded into misery all those months ago.

I rushed over to where they stood, and Mama threw her arms around me, hugging me to her tightly. "Oh Neely," she gasped, pulling back so she could look me over, "I'm so happy you decided to come home early. Aren't we happy, Mama?" she asked, glancing over at Grandma.

"Well, we surely are," my grandmother replied. "Is everything okay with you, Neilah?" she asked, her forehead creased with concern.

"Oh, yes, Grandma. Just homesick I guess."

"Well of course you were, darlin'," Mama said, wrapping an arm around my shoulder as we walked towards the escalator that would take us to the lower level to Baggage Claim. "Why, a whole month away from your family is just too much. I was sick with worry about you, wasn't I Mama?"

My grandmother gave a nod, which told me that Mama had likely been hitting the bottle again.

"Tell me, Neilah Grace, tell me the truth. Did your father bring that whore around you while you were there? Did he?"

I stopped and turned to her. "No, Mama. He did not. I mostly hung out with Seth. I never saw Tiffany Blume, I swear it."

I saw her visibly relax. "Well, at least he hasn't totally lost his mind, I guess. Did he ask about me, Neely? Your daddy--did he want to know how I was?"

We started walking again, getting onto the downward escalator. "Sure he did," I lied, "and I told him you were just fine, Mama."

"Well good for you," she replied, laughing. "I'm betting he regrets the day he ever set eyes on

Tiffany Blume. Yes sir, he is surely realizing just how much his infidelity has cost him now!"

I looked up at my grandmother who had just stepped onto the escalator. Our eyes met and she shook her head back and forth as if she'd been listening to this kind of talk from Mama the whole time I'd been gone. She probably had been. I could only imagine how my Mama's manic behavior had grated on their nerves. It had become a pattern with Mama. Always manic before the despair settled in again.

"Neely, honey," my mama piped up, "I want you to promise me you won't go back there next summer. I just can't take it when you leave me like that. I did nothing but fret over you the whole time. If your daddy wants to see you, let him take time off and come out here. He can stay at a hotel and visit with you here in Tennessee. You tell him that, okay?"

"Okay, Mama," I said with a sigh. "I'll let him know."

"And tell him not to bring that slut with him either. I don't want the likes of her around you. You tell him that too, okay?"

"I will, Mama. I promise. I will."

We waited about ten minutes until my luggage came down the chute and landed on the moving carousel. Mama picked up one of the suitcases, and I grabbed the other.

"Your granddaddy is out front with the car. He's gonna drive us to our new place, honey. Grandma helped me get settled in. You're going to love our new apartment. It's an old Victorian house on a well-maintained street with lots and lots of shade trees."

"It sounds nice, Mama," I replied, as we stepped outside the terminal and the hot humidity of Tennessee assaulted us. "Wow, so different than California weather," I commented.

"Of course it is. Much better, don't you think?" she asked. "But don't worry. Our apartment has window air conditioners. We'll be comfortable there. Oh, and I got a job!" she squealed, clapping her hands together. "I got a job as a receptionist with a lawyer downtown. Isn't that exciting?"

"Yes, Mama. That is fantastic news," I replied, trying to sound enthused.

The ride to our new apartment from the airport went achingly slow. I wasn't in the mood for conversation.

My head was throbbing from the plane trip, and the fact that my father had been confused and angry when I told him I needed to go home immediately because my mother needed me.

It hadn't totally been a lie. When I had called Mama once I'd gotten back to Daddy's house to see if she could pick me up at the airport, she had truly sobbed in happiness that I was coming back early. She went on and on telling me how miserable she'd been since I'd gone to visit him, and how much she needed me back there where I belonged.

"Neely, the court says I have you for a month. It's been just two weeks, I--"

"Daddy, I need to go home now. Are you gonna take me to the airport, or do you want me to call a cab?" I'd interrupted, getting mouthy which was something I'd never done before.

"Fine!" he'd spat. "Get in the car. I'll take this up with my lawyer."

And so he'd driven me to the airport in silence. Content with being angry with my mother who he blamed for my early departure. I allowed him to believe that because it was easier. Yeah, it was a shitty thing to do, but at that point, I couldn't deal with baring my soul to anyone. Not even him.

And my heart ached knowing that I wouldn't go back next year, partly because Mama had begged me not to leave her like that again, but mostly because I couldn't face Seth after leaving the ring and the note for him like a coward.

But it had been the right thing to do for everyone concerned. I was too young to feel this way. Too young to commit to anyone emotionally.

I had a lot to figure out on my own. I doubted if Mama was going to be of any help, so it was up to me to sort things out. To make the best choices and decisions I could at my age, and to learn from past experiences and mistakes going forward.

The ache in my heart would eventually diminish. I would start at a new school in a few weeks, which would hopefully be full of new promises for me.

A clean slate.

A blank canvas.

A fresh start.

"Mama," I said as my grandfather pulled off the interstate and on to our exit, "did you find all my art supplies? My paints, brushes, and canvases? I think I want to start painting again."

"Well, I'm sure they are there, honey. We've got at least twenty boxes left to unpack. We'll get to it as soon as we get home, how's that? What're you thinking about painting?"

"I'm not sure, Mama. I'm thinking about getting into some expressionist art."

"Expressionist?" she asked, her forehead creasing in confusion. Mama didn't know much about various art themes or styles. "What's that?"

"It's kind of hard to explain," I replied. "It's sort of like taking a subject, and painting it in a distorted way. Making it more of an emotional expression on the canvas versus the physical reality of it. Making it totally subjective."

"I see," she replied. "Well, who will your subject be in your first painting, Neely?"

"That's easy," I replied with a pensive smile. "Seth Drake. He'll be the perfect subject for my very first oil expressionist painting."

The End of Book 1

How About a Sneak Peak of Book 2?

Here's an excerpt from Book 2 in the Evermore Series, entitled "Claimed"

"Neely," Professor Andrews said, gazing at the collage I'd placed on the wooden easel for my presentation, "that's a very interesting choice of media you've selected. Not to mention risky."

"Risky?" I asked, quirking a brow in confusion. "How so?"

"Well, to start, you veered a bit from the assignment details which clearly articulated that everything was to be in black, white, or shades of grey. The lack of contrast was important. You've included some color in your abstracts."

"Only the eyes, Professor," I replied, standing back and admiring my work. "I couldn't bear not to show the ice blue of the eyes. It doesn't detract from the overall message though, does it?"

I watched as Professor Andrews cupped his chin, rubbing his fingers along the bristle of his neatly trimmed beard and considered my expressionist collage thoughtfully.

When he'd give this particular assignment, it had taken me all of a nanosecond to know which of my pieces I'd be using to compile the collage of emotional turmoil he'd outlined. And yes, I'd known that it was supposed to be void of color, but the eyes wouldn't have shown the emotion had I not brushed a pale shade of blue over them.

"I'll tell you what, Neely," he said, "stay after class and let's discuss this in a bit more depth, shall we?"

"Of course," I replied, taking my seat so that the next presenter could uncover his or her submission for this assignment. This was the third class in two years at Brantley School of Art & Photography I'd taken with Eric Andrews as my professor.

I knew him well. He was a superb teacher in every way. And yes, he was a stickler for adherence to detail on the projects he outlined and assigned for his classes, but he was also a fair and flexible man. Let's just say, we'd had issues like this before and always found common ground.

I'd stay after as requested. He'd pull a copy of the assignment details he'd provided to all of the students four weeks ago, and go over each one with me, point-by-point.

I'd sit at my table and remain silent as he ticked through each one, his deep, rich voice resonating the fact that he indeed had the upper hand in deciding whether or not my submission which had, technically, strayed from the parameters he'd set, would be accepted for credit.

In the end, he would allow me time to explain my reasoning for veering from the instructions, and defend my position as to why I felt it still complied with the overall spirit of the assignment, and therefore should be accepted for grading and credit.

He would ultimately concede, with a stern warning that I needed to focus more on adherence on future assignments. I would thank him for his consideration and flexibility, to which he would chuckle and tell me that it was now my turn to be flexible.

At that point, he would make sure the door to the art room was shut and locked. And then, he would pull me up from my seat against him. I would wrap my legs around his hips and allow him to carry me to a table or desktop, or maybe to a paint-splattered tarp that was heaped into a corner of the room. Whatever location he chose was where I would show him my flexibility.

Clothes would hurriedly be discarded in a frenzied fashion, and he would take me roughly, which I always demanded, and we'd fuck until we couldn't fuck anymore.

I knew the script by heart. We'd played to it more than once. Probably more like a dozen times over the past year. It still wasn't boring. Neither of us had grown tired of the foreplay we called Perspective Painting 201.

Everything unraveled just as usual. The classroom emptied, a couple of students lagged behind to suck up to him for projects presented this evening that were less than stellar. It was always pretty obvious. Eric did his best to assure them he would be fair and objective in his evaluation of their work.

Sure he would.

They were slackers.

They only took this class because they were required to as part of the curriculum for their Graphic Web Design certificate program. They had zero interest in art, expression, or theory.

At last.

We were alone.

Eric shut and locked the classroom door, and then quickly stalked over to where I was still sitting, gazing up at him. He was strikingly handsome with perfectly chiseled features and a great body definition for a man whose career didn't involve physical labor of any sort. Dark brown hair and eyes. Thirtyish with a scholarly look that his dark-framed glasses perpetuated nicely.

"So, Professor," I said in a throaty whisper. "Shall we debate the particulars of my non-compliance to the assignment once again?"

He didn't move any closer to me. In fact, he leaned back against the table in front of my desk, and stretched his legs out in front of him. His arms were crossed against his chest and he gazed at me for a moment, not saying a word.

This was different.

For a moment I worried if quite possibly he wasn't open to our usual negotiations. He surely wouldn't fail me on this assignment, would he?

"Why him?" he asked me, his eyes searching mine. "Why is it always him?"

"Wh-what?" I asked, my nose crinkled up in confusion. He was deviating from our normal script. What the hell was up with that? "I'm...I'm not following."

"For Chrissake, Neely. No matter what the assignment, the required subject matter, the requested media, every goddamn one of your projects has some part of him included. Be it an eye, or lips, or a nose, or a full fucking face, it's always him. Why?"

"Why does it matter?" I flung back. "Art is subjective, right? Maybe he's my art. Maybe he's the only subject matter I've ever done right."

"So what? You simply keep drawing and painting him--or parts of him, over and over again in different themes, different styles, with different media rather than try something new? Something unique?"

I stood up quickly. "Every piece I've turned in to you has been freshly created! It's all been unique! It's not as if I keep turning the same pieces in over and over again, is it?" I was pissed now. What the hell was Eric trying to do? Why was he straying from the script?

"You might as well be turning the same piece in over and over again!" he shouted, startling me enough that I jumped. "I want you to turn something in, anything, that he's not a goddamn part of!"

I was shocked by his words, stunned by his anger. I backed away from where he sat, one arm outstretched behind me to make sure I didn't collide with a desk. "I don't understand. Why are you so angry with me, Eric?" I whispered.

He ran a hand through his mass of thick hair as if frustrated beyond his limit. "I'm not angry, Neely, I'm confused. Who the hell is this guy to you?"

I felt my muscles tense. My stomach clenched. I didn't have to share any of this with Eric Andrews. He had no right to even question me about it. It wasn't any of his business. His job was to teach and offer guidance and support for his students. His job was most certainly not to try to get into my head or to figure out what makes me tick, or why I chose the subject matter I did for my projects.

That was my shrink's job, right?

"Listen," I said, my voice holding a nervous lilt. "Are you going to accept my submission for this assignment or not? I need to know."

He blinked a couple of times, still studying me as if his reading glasses had suddenly morphed into a powerful microscope that was unpeeling each and every layer of my psyche for his own personal examination.

"Yes," he finally said, releasing a heavy sigh. "It's accepted for grade."

"Okay then," I whispered, still watching him, a feeling of relief seeping over me. "So, are we going to fuck?"

He removed his glasses, and rubbed the bridge of his nose with his fingers, massaging away his obvious frustration. "No, Neely. No we're not."

I shrugged and grabbed my backpack from the top of my desk, and hoisted it up and over my shoulders. "Goodnight then, Eric. See you in class tomorrow," I replied as I left his classroom and headed out of the building.

It was just as well we stopped having sex anyway, I thought to myself as I walked along the paved parking lot toward my car. It had run its course, and in the scheme of things, it wasn't a long-term fit. I'd already concluded that a while back. Now I could focus fully on my curriculum.

My next semester's course load was going to be a killer. But I relished the challenge. I longed for anything and everything to occupy a place in my mind. Thankfully, this would be my last class under Professor Andrews.

Literally.

End of excerpt from **"Claimed"**

Releases August of 2016

How About a YA Suspense Teaser?

Southern Comfort by Andrea Smith

Prologue

Growing up in central Alabama had its perks believe it or not. Especially if you lived in rural Alabama, better known as the "sticks."

Oh, I knew that most teenage girls wouldn't feel that way, in particular if they were used to city life, whether big or small. I can tell you they might feel differently if they'd lived the first seventeen years of their lives in Layton, Alabama like me.

I was the second child born to my mother and husband number two. My older brother, Jamie, had done the smart thing and joined the military as soon as he hit eighteen. That had been my plan as well, only things happened before I turned eighteen that changed everything. Layton, like all towns, had its secrets. For only having a population of eleven thousand, the secrets per capita were astronomical.

But don't go looking for Layton, Alabama on some map because you won't find it. You see, it actually doesn't exist.

Well, it *exists*.

It just doesn't exist under *that* particular name. Yeah, I changed the name of the small rural town where I lived for the first seventeen years of my life in order to protect…the guilty.

And let me tell you, once you have read my story you'll understand that for yourself. In the interest of honesty, I admit that I was no angel, but who at seventeen was? I considered myself average behavior-wise. I was no goody two-shoes, but I also wasn't a total rebellious chick by any means.

I didn't put on false airs, or try to come off as some holier than thou person, unlike my thrice married mama. She thought she had everyone fooled. Married to husband number three, which happened to be one of the local preachers, had done a lot to repair her reputation in the community. That was one of the nice things about living in Layton. Folks there were more than happy to forgive, once you aired your dirty laundry for all to see.

And they loved Preacher Dawson. At least, they loved the man they saw every Sunday in the pulpit; the man of cloth that presented himself as a God-fearing instrument of the Almighty. The man that cleansed the souls of the young and the old down on the banks of the Tahatchapee River once a month when baptisms were conducted. The man that led the prayer at the monthly church picnics.

But that's not really who he was; it was only who he pretended to be. If the people in this sleepy southern town knew the real man beneath his black garb and wide-brimmed preacher's hat, they most surely would have locked their doors at night and changed their religious denomination.

No one believed that I would ever return to Layton after the scandal that had erupted nearly a year ago. At least my reckless naiveté taught me how to tough it out in order to survive, negotiate with evil when I had to, and learn to shrug off the ugliness and not let it become a part of me. I had no choice if I were to survive.

My mother had simply turned a blind eye to it all. She thought she was playing it safe, being the loyal and supportive preacher's wife. In Avery Dawson, she felt she had met her one true love. Unlike husbands one and two, Avery was not only ambrosia for her heart, he was also manna for her soul. Yeah, Mama's thing had always been taking the path of least resistance, even if it meant enduring the unthinkable, which eventually she would because of Avery Dawson and his pernicious soul.

My brother was smart to get the hell out of Layton after Avery came into our lives. Me, on the other hand, I reacted the only way I knew how at sixteen. I lived on the edge, occasionally pushing my limits at home and at school. Life for me had become about avoiding my home life once Avery became part of it. My mama might have been inclined to turn a blind eye to his evil, but I wasn't allowed that luxury once the truth hit me square in the face.

My story is about when they did. About when the truth about Avery Dawson came to light with his congregation witnessing the proof of his evil ways. Sure, I had helped with exposing him for the hypocrite that he was, but how could I have known how far Avery would go in his duplicitous ways? Even my own mother had betrayed me, spreading lies and turning the town against me so that Avery would continue to be held in high esteem.

Her own damn daughter.

And now I have some unfinished business back in Layton, Alabama. I'm eighteen and the year I've spent away has given me the courage to find out the truth about myself and, in doing so, I found out so much more. Maybe I did flee in shame a year ago, but I've learned a lot since then and the truth, however unpalatable it might be, has given me the raw courage and determination to set the record straight.

I think it's about time that I show my face again, and deal with the people I left in my wake. The people that claim to be Born Again Christians in one breath, and in the next pointing accusatory fingers at those who are innocent, and deny the truth when it smacks them in the face.

In Layton, they are big on forgiveness. But the thing is? I'm not looking for forgiveness. All I want is vindication.

CHAPTER 1

Eighteen months earlier…

Summer of 1979

The sun had left the sky as the blue Mercury Marquis pulled into the winding drive leading up to the ticket booth. The car slowed as it took its place in line. The radio was blasting the newest Rolling Stones tune and I watched as Gina expertly lit her cigarette with one hand while she rolled her window down with the other.

In the back seat, Rene and Robin were still arguing as to whose turn it was to pay for their tickets into the drive-in movie. It was a "twin thing," I had learned, and it was best not to get into the middle of it.

Gina coasted up to the ticket window, and flashed her sweetest smile to the cashier. He was wearing a gold shirt, and a small black bow tie. There was a plastic nametag pinned on the pocket of his shirt. Jerry. He was probably in college, working at the drive-in for the summer to help with his tuition. He didn't appear too impressed with Gina's smile and glanced surreptitiously into the car for a quick scan of the occupants.

"Sorry, girls. No can do. The movies are rated "X" and that means eighteen years of age or older."

Gina took a slow, long drag off of her cigarette, French inhaling, and gave him a flirtatious smile. "Aww, c'mon Jerry. I'm eighteen, see?" she replied, flipping out her driver's license to show him.

"What about the rest of you?" he asked, peering back inside of the car. Got I.D.'s?

"Aww, come on now, sugar. We won't tell if you won't." Her New Jersey accent was endearing to us Southerners, and I was always amazed at how worldly it made her sound.

She had moved back from Hoboken a few years ago after her parents had split. She still went back every summer to spend a month with her dad. This was her first week back.

"I'm sorry," Jerry responded, irritation mounting, "but rules are rules. Now you need to turn the vehicle around on the right and head out so the cars behind you can get in."

Gina, not one to give up, stubbed her cigarette out in the ashtray, making sure that her candy-red nails remained ashless. She turned her full attention to Jerry. She leaned out the window, allowing him clear view of her ample cleavage from his vantage point. The white halter top she was wearing showed off her beautifully tanned skin, and accentuated her dark brown eyes. Her eyebrows, always perfectly plucked in a Scarlet O'Hara arch, now moved into a slight frown.

"But Jerry," she cooed, "what we got here are four girls on a Saturday night, just looking to see a movie. Now you're not going to spoil our night out by being some stickler, are you?"

Gina reached into her halter top and pulled out a wad of bills. "Hey, I bet you could use a nice tip for the great job you do, how about it?"

Jerry was now flustered, but his eyes widened nonetheless. I wasn't sure if that was because he got a nice glimpse of Gina's boobs or if he was impressed with the wad of cash she pulled out. Gina rifled through the bills with one long, red fingernail, and I saw at least four ten dollar bills flash by before she stopped and pulled them out, folded them over and then stuck them in Jerry's front pocket with a wink.

"There ya go, doll," she purred flirtatiously.

Jerry wasn't sure what to think. Neither was I. He finally stepped back to the booth and returned with four tickets, handing them through the window to Gina.

"Thanks, doll," she giggled, and the car lurched forward.

"Geez, when did you get rich? I asked.

"My dad, Sunny, ya know how it is. The parents, they're all like guilty when they split for the rest of their lives apparently."

No, I didn't know. The truth was, I hadn't seen my father since Mama divorced him years ago. He lived in Chicago now. Mama said he had a new wife. The most he did was to pay child support. My brother had a different dad. I can't recall him being a part of his life, either. I suppose whenever Mama cut a husband loose, they made tracks fast.

"Hey Sunny!" Rene shouted from the back seat over the music. "Are you still going with me to pick out something to wear to Randy's party?"

I turned my attention to the back seat while Gina searched up and down the various rows for the best space to park. Robin and Rene Marshall were twins, and while they shared identical features, their tastes in boys, clothes, and music were worlds apart. This was why either one of them always asked either Gina or myself to help with those decisions. Randy was Rene's steady boyfriend. He would be turning eighteen the week before we started our senior year of high school.

"I can," I replied, "as long as it's after work."

I worked a part-time summer job at the local Tastee-Freez. I did it for the money and to get out of the house as much as possible. My friends considered it a burden for them. They couldn't fathom any teenager wanting to work during the summer. But I actually enjoyed the work and having my own money. That was the only way I would have any spending money since Mama didn't believe in giving an allowance. Well, I think she did, but since she'd remarried, I noticed things she used to do for fun and for me disappeared, little by little.

"Well, how late are you working Monday? I want to get something before the stores all put their winter clothes out, ya know?"

"I'm off at three," I replied.

"Good." Rene was pleased. "I'll pick you up at three then."

"What about you, Robin?" I asked. "Are you coming with us?"

"No fucking way," she replied, rolling her eyes. "She drives me nuts with her shopping. The dance is lame. I've got other plans for that night."

"Better hope the parents don't find out," Rene chided. I was sure I'd hear all about Robin's plans while shopping. Those two were certainly a trip. Both were blonde, blue-eyed, and petite. In my world that was the whole package.

As for me, I was considered average height at 5'6" and my friends claimed they envied my build, but really, I didn't give a shit about that stuff. I considered myself average on all fronts. But, at almost seventeen, my goal was to surpass average on some level or another.

My height was average, my build was average, my looks were average, and my intelligence was average. Perhaps my life was destined for mediocrity.

My mother's vanity was enough for the both of us. She loved when people at church commented that we looked like sisters instead of mother and daughter. She had my older brother when she was just eighteen, and I came along three years later. At thirty-eight she took pains to make sure every hair was in place, and every nail was painted perfectly.

She borrowed my makeup and clothes, which, as a preacher's wife, I found to be a bit…unconventional, if not objectionable, although Avery didn't seem to object as long as she presented herself more conservatively when she attended church services.

Preacher or not, a man was a man. No matter what their vocation, they all wanted a pretty woman on their arm. That's what Mama said anyway. And a woman's job was to make sure to please her man or else he'd stray. She wasn't about to let that happen with the best 'catch' of Compton County. They had only been married for a year and my eighteenth birthday wouldn't get here soon enough. But first I had to hit my seventeenth birthday.

"I love your eyes," Gina said out of the blue ones glancing over at me. It was almost as if she'd been tuned into my thoughts. "They're such a fucking pretty shade of blue. They're like blue ice…ya know? Like a Siberian Husky. I hate my eyes. I'm just so average."

See what I mean? Telepathic was the word.

There was nothing average about Gina. She was just a bit shorter than me, and built like the proverbial brick shit-house. She had gorgeous and flawless olive skin, obviously passed through her Italian ancestors. Gina was way bustier than any of us, with size Double D cups as she liked to remind us as often as possible.

Her mom had remarried since they moved back here. Her stepfather, Eddie Sanders, made good money at the factory where he worked. Gina had turned eighteen this past March. She was the oldest in our group. She'd been held back a year in first grade, so we were all going into our senior year. I would turn seventeen in September, and the twins would catch up with me in October.

Gina's mom, Gloria, was a hair stylist in town. Gloria had grown up in Layton, but they'd moved to New Jersey when Gina's dad had been transferred there when she'd been a baby. Having a hair stylist as a mother had its perks. Gina always presented the newest hairstyles and manicures as a result. Her mom didn't load her down with a lot of chores or rules. She was a free spirit and that was what made her so much fun. My mother didn't necessarily approve of Gina, although she had never articulated why. I think it was because Avery didn't approve of her. He was very outspoken on things like that but he had only met Gina a handful of times. Mama explained that Avery's gift was the ability to assess one's soul in a matter of minutes.

Gina pulled her mom's Mercury into a parking spot and, as luck would have it, the speaker was on my side. Crap! I hated the feeling of being blocked in.

I was majorly claustrophobic so I guess that was why. I pulled the speaker off the rack on the post outside of the window, and hung it carefully on the glass rolled halfway down on my door. The Top 40 chart was blaring from the speaker, and I adjusted the sound down a bit.

The Showboat Drive-In was the last in the county. At one time, there had been two other drive-in movie theatres in the area, but those had closed up years back. The Showboat was notorious for playing X-rated movies and, like any teenagers, we were curious.

Except for Gina. Gina was actually the only one in our group who had experienced sex. Though she was always more than happy to share every detail with us, the movies gave us much more explicit detail than even Gina could.

This film was classic John Holmes. Not much of a plot, but it was obvious where Mr. Holmes' talent resided. All sixteen freaking inches of it!

In this flick, Holmes was playing the owner of a plastics company that was introducing a new dildo line. He was encouraged to demonstrate the dildo in a comparison test with his own member. Geez!

Rene was aghast in the back seat.

"Oh my God," she screeched. "That cannot be real!"

Robin shushed her as Holmes continued his demo on his buxom secretary from behind. The secretary was making the appropriate moans and groans as he finally succeeded in burying his full length into her.

"Ouch!" Gina screamed. "Ain't no freakin' way, baby!"

The dudes in the car next to us were laughing. The driver looked over at us and stared a hole through me. "Hey there sweet thing," he crooned. "Why don't you come on over here and I can show you a rod bigger than that and all the magic things it can do for you?"

"Jack off, jerk!" I responded and then turned to Gina. "Why in the hell did you park next to these idiots, Gina?"

"Oh, hell, Sunny. Be cool. They're just horny like the rest of us. Don't be so uptight all the time. God, who would've guessed your stepdaddy has already infiltrated your bad self," she finished with a laugh.

"First of all," I answered, trying not to be irritated, "I really don't know what horny feels like. And secondly, my stepfather is a jerk and I'll thank you not to mention him if you want to remain friends, that is. And lastly, I'm not uptight just because I haven't chosen to screw someone yet, okay?"

Gina was my best friend and I loved her "like a sis," but she had already shared with me that she lost her cherry when she was fourteen to a guy named Dennis. He promised her it wouldn't hurt and it had. He promised her that it would clear up her complexion. Well, her complexion cleared up once her mom had taken her to a dermatologist who prescribed some tetracycline. So, I guess Gina pretty much had been played the fool. But all in all, she seemed to have taken it in stride.

Dennis had not been the last. She had recently broken up with a guy named Larry that was a few years older than her and worked at the lumberyard. Gina said that Larry just didn't "get her," and she was ready to explore other options.

I thanked God that Gina's mom had the foresight to put her on birth control pills when she was fifteen, though Gina seemed very touchy about the whole subject.

Regrettably, I made the mistake of mentioning this to my mother one day and sat through one of her horrible, fire and brimstone, if not totally hypocritical lectures on acceptable behavior. "Obviously, Sunny, Gina is not a product of proper breeding," she had said, fanning herself with a Penny Dreadful she'd been reading. "I'm half tempted to forbid you from associating with her. You are, after all, judged by the company you keep. Do you want folks around here thinking you're...well, some kind of *white trash?*"

"No, but Gina is not trash, Mama. She's my best friend and if I can't talk to you about things without you starting to pass judgment, then I just won't share stuff with you at all. Is that how you want it?" Sometimes turning the tables on her worked to my advantage. I was hoping that this was one of those times.

She'd grown flustered and, thankfully, the phone rang right then killing the conversation. Still, I could tell that she wasn't happy having Gina around after that. It was clearly evident the next time Gina had come to the house.

"What's your mom's freakin' problem today?" Gina had asked. My mother had barely returned Gina's greeting when she stopped by to pick me up for a trip to the mall.

167

"Just ignore it," I had responded casually. "She's just mad at me and when that happens, she takes it out on everyone associated with me. C'mon, let's split."

"Aw, shit!" Gina said, breaking into my momentary reflection. "I freakin' forgot to put the cooler with the Little Kings in the backseat. It's still in the trunk. Rene, I'll pop the trunk, jump out and grab the cooler, huh?"

Rene scrambled out of the back seat as Gina popped the massive trunk open, blocking the view for the car parked directly behind us. Rene was apparently having some difficulty in locating the cooler, which was usually well hidden under several blankets Gina kept back there for her impromptu picnics with her dates.

"Hey, you dumb bitch, close the fucking trunk so we can see the flick!"

"Shut your damn face!" Gina screamed right back at the car behind us filled with guys, obviously not intimidated whatsoever. She poked her head out of the car window while giving them the one finger salute in a rotational manner.

I heard more cursing and a car door slammed behind us. Rene hurriedly shut the lid of trunk, and barreled into the backseat with the cooler in tow.

She was laughing loudly as she pulled the car door shut and pushed down the lock.

Oh, geez, what now?

I slumped down low in the front seat, while Gina flung her door wide open, and jumped out facing the tall, blonde-haired dude that sported a tattooed arm and was carrying a can of Bud with him.

As soon as he eyed Gina, he visibly cooled off. Standing with her arms akimbo in cut-off shorts, white halter top, which did little to conceal her double D's, and brown eyes blazing she presented a rather lusty dilemma for the blonde hot head.

"Hey, look," he mumbled sheepishly now, "sorry for getting loud with your friend there. Lemme make it up to you. Want a beer?"

Damn.

I peeked out through Gina's window and it almost looked like he was blushing. Gina could affect guys that way. Me--I could never pull that off. Not in a million years.

"Nah, we're good here. Rene was just getting our refreshments outta the trunk. Sorry we blocked your view like that."

"No, no, *I'm* sorry for going all radical like that. Hey, my name is Craig," he offered, wiping his right hand on his jeans before offering it to Gina. "Craig Connors at your beck and call, Ms...?"

Gina shrugged and with a dazzling smile offered her manicured hand to him almost daintily. It always amazed me the way that she could quickly transform herself from a hardened Jersey chick into a soft picture of feminine refinement.

"Gina," she said softly. "My name is Gina Margolis."

"Well, Gina Margolis," Craig continued, "are you sure there isn't something I can offer you--popcorn, a corn dog, a joint, anything? I was an ass."

"Why yes, yes you *were*, Craig," she scolded half-heartedly, "and how un-Southern that was, but really, it's no big deal. Tell you what, check back at intermission if you want. I may have some needs then," she chuckled.

She turned and got back into the car as Craig made no attempt to hide the fact he was checking her out from behind. He let out a soft wolf-whistle before he turned and went back to his car.

"Oh my God!" she giggled as she watched it all in her rearview mirror. "Is he not the most beautiful thing you've seen all day? God, I love guys with tats!"

"Gina, you love guys with tats, moles, scars, zits, limps. What is your point?" Robin asked, twisting the top off of her chilled bottle of Little King Cream Ale. "I mean, the fact is you LOVE guys. Period."

"Stop being nasty, Robin," Gina chided, "or I won't ask Craig if he has a friend for you at intermission."

They both laughed while Rene tossed each of us a bottle of ale. I twisted the cap off of mine and took a long draw. I had to admit, I really don't care for the taste of cream ale, but it was hot and I was thirsty. So it would have to do for now.

I knew that I would nurse it through the rest of the movie. What the hell? There were only a total of eight so no one would be getting drunk anyway. The best we could hope for was that good 'ole Craig came through with a doobie at intermission.

We got back to watching Johnny Wadd Holmes and his weapon of doom as Gina called it, making appropriate comments throughout. At one point, Robin put us into a fit of giggles when she said watching him screw his nurse was giving her a tingling feeling between her legs.

Gina snorted out ale through her nose on that one. "Are you for real, Robin? I mean I get that three outta the four of us are virgins, but shit, come on. There are three bases in between, ya know?"

Here we go. Time for an update.

"Time for an update!" Gina yelled. "You first, Sunny. Tell us, Ms. Gardner, how you've spent *your* summer vacation."

I rolled my eyes, taking another swig of my drink. "You know damn well nothing's changed this summer, Gina. Still me. No boyfriend. No contenders on the horizon. Everything still intact here."

"Yeah, figured that," she said with a sigh of disappointment. "Twins?"

"Nothing new with me either, guys are jerks as far as I'm concerned. Rene got finger banged by Randy though."

"Robin! Shut up! That was for me to tell!"

"Oh what's the big deal?" Robin replied. "You said it wasn't all that, anyway."

Gina turned abruptly to face Rene. "What's the skinny with that? You didn't enjoy it?"

Now Rene was in the hot seat. I turned to see how she was gonna react.

She squirmed uncomfortably and then smacked her twin on the shoulder. "See?"

"Hey, I'm not here to judge, just curious," Gina said. "So did Randy not know the basics of finger fucking or what?"

"Well, it started out okay. I mean, you know, we were making out and all, and then he was feeling me up, and then down my shorts and all, but no – it didn't feel good. It was something about the angle I guess. I mean, hell, his knuckles were pressed up against my vagina and it hurt."

"Oh, for Pete's sake," Gina replied, shaking her head. "No wonder. That isn't the correct position for a successful finger bang. You were sitting up, right?"

Rene nodded.

"That is totally wrong. You need to be lying down, naked from the waist down, and your legs relaxed. He needs to take his time, get you kind of lathered up, and then gently ply the folds of your dirty girl and work it from there."

"Dirty girl?" I gasped, spitting out the sip of ale I had just taken.

Gina turned back to face me. "Okay, what would you prefer I call it? Vagina? Don't think so."

"Pussy," I replied without thinking.

"Ewww," Robin said from the back seat. "I hate that word!"

"It's better than 'dirty girl,'" I argued. "That just sounds nasty."

"The point is," Gina clarified loudly, "that he didn't know what the hell he was doing. Is he still a virgin?"

"Well…yeah," Rene said. "We both are."

"Then take my advice and try the position I just explained. And here's a hot tip: once he's got two fingers up inside, have him curl them up like he's beckoning you, and wait until you feel the fireworks hit!"

I smiled, shaking my head. Gina. Something else. "Which one are you?" I asked her.

"Huh?"

"I'm asking which one you are – Masters or Johnson?"

"Fuck you, Sunny."

ABOUT THE AUTHOR

Andrea Smith is a USA Today and Amazon Best-Selling Author of the G-Man Series! She has a wicked sense of humor, and no matter the genre, she is able to infuse laughter throughout.

She self-publishes Contemporary Romance, Romantic Suspense, and Sensual Romance with a paranormal twist. She also writes New Adult Romance, and has recently collaborated with Author Eva LeNoir on two M/M Romances, with the third releasing Fall 2016!

Here is a listing of her published fiction to date:

Baby Series (New Adult Romance/Suspense)

These Books should be read in order:

Maybe Baby (Book 1)

Baby Love   (Book 2)

Be My Baby (Book 3)

Baby Come Back (Novella) (Book 3.5)

G-Man Series (Contemporary Romance/Suspense)

Can be standalones, but are most enjoyable if read in order.

Diamond Girl (Book 1)

Love Plus One (Book 2)

Night Moves   (Book 3)

G-Men Holiday Wrap (Novella) (Book 3.5)

These Men (Spin-off) Part of the BEND anthology. (M/F/M)

My Men (Sequel to "These Men") (M/F/M)

Taz (G-Man Book 4)

G-Man: Next Generation (New Adult Romance)

Walk of Shame (Book 1)

WTF? Series

Jaded

Limbo Series (Contemporary Steamy Romance)

Silent Whisper

Clouds in My Coffee

September Series (New Adult- Taboo)

Need to be read in order.

Until September   (Book 1)

When September Ends   (Book 2)

M/M Romance

Black Balled (Co-Authored with Eva LeNoir)

Guns Blazing (Spin-Off from Black Balled)

Hard Edit (Sequel to "Black Balled" with Eva LeNoir)

<u>YA Suspense</u>

Southern Comfort

<u>Social Media Links:</u>

To sign up for her monthly newsletter, visit her website: http://www.andreasmithauthor.com/

Stalk her on Facebook:

https://www.facebook.com/AndreaSmithAuthor/

Follow her on Twitter:

https://twitter.com/GManAuthor

GOODREADS:

https://www.goodreads.com/author/show/6869343.Andrea_Smith

66117288R00100

Made in the USA
Charleston, SC
12 January 2017